The Martian Simulacra

NewCon Novellas

Set 1: *(Cover art by Chris Moore)*
    The Iron Tactician – Alastair Reynolds
    At the Speed of Light – Simon Morden
    The Enclave – Anne Charnock
    The Memoirist – Neil Williamson

Set 2: *(Cover art by Vincent Sammy)*
    Sherlock Holmes: Case of the Bedevilled Poet – Simon Clark
    Cottingley – Alison Littlewood
    The Body in the Woods – Sarah Lotz
    The Wind – Jay Caselberg

Set 3: *(Cover art by Jim Burns)*
    The Martian Job – Jaine Fenn
    Sherlock Holmes: The Martian Simulacra – Eric Brown
    Phosphorous: A Winterstrike Story – Liz Williams
    The Greatest Story Ever Told – Una McCormack

The Martian Simulacra

A Sherlock Holmes Mystery

Eric Brown

NewCon Press
England

First published in the UK by NewCon Press
41 Wheatsheaf Road, Alconbury Weston, Cambs, PE28 4LF
January 2018

NCP 139 (limited edition hardback)
NCP 140 (softback)

10 9 8 7 6 5 4 3 2 1

ISBN:

978-1-910935-63-7 (hardback)
978-1-910935-64-4 (softback)

Cover art by Jim Burns
Cover layout by Ian Whates

Minor Editorial meddling by Ian Whates
Book layout by Storm Constantine

One

A Visitor to 221B Baker Street

In 1907, one year after my friend's involvement in what became known as the Tragic Affair of the Martian Ambassador, Sherlock Holmes was once again called upon to render assistance to our extraterrestrial overlords.

In the interim, Holmes had worked on just one case, an inquiry so trifling I elected not to add it to the already copious annals of his exploits: it was at the request of an old acquaintance that he solved the theft of a priceless diamond tiara, an investigation which taxed him for a mere two days. For the most part his time had been spent conducting a series of chemical experiments, studying his twelve volume set of the *Encyclopaedia Martiannica*, and scanning the crime pages of the *London Gazette*. Often, late into the evening over a glass of brandy, he would regale me with what he had learned of Martian life from the encyclopaedia, as well as offering his own solutions to the crimes and scandals of the day.

I, for my part, divided my time between my club and a select group of private patients in west London. I was well into my sixth decade, and slowing down; the old war injury was troubling me from time to time, and my concentration was not what it had been. Holmes upbraided me on this score: "What you should be doing, Watson, is not so much slowing down but speeding up."

"What on earth do you mean, Holmes?"

He examined me over his toast; it was a brilliant summer's morning, not yet eight o'clock, and through the windows of 221B Baker Street I looked out upon yet another cloudless day. To the north, the cowl of a Martian tripod towered, silent and brooding, over Regent's Park.

"People of our age often make the mistake of thinking that they should reward themselves – grant themselves a gift for long-service, as it were – by 'slowing down'." He pointed a thin finger at me. "But this is lazy thinking. Only by keeping active, physically and mentally, can we hope to keep senility and decrepitude at bay."

"That's all very well for you to say," I retorted, "the possessor of a relatively healthy body and a brilliant mind."

"I appreciate your war injury, Watson, but what I suggest is that you take up a hobby, embark on something new and mentally invigorating."

I blustered and feigned absorption in *The Times*. "You're probably right," I said.

The arrival of the Martians ten years earlier had prompted Holmes to teach himself the fundamentals of their complex language; he had mastered their tongue in a matter of three years, and not only was he now one of the few human beings fluent in demotic Martianese, but he was proficient in the classical form of their language as spoken by the aristocracy of the Red Planet.

As if this were not enough, Holmes had thrown himself into studying the basics of Martian sciences, or rather what crumbs of knowledge our overlords allowed to fall from the banqueting table of their vast scientific and philosophical feast.

"But dash it all, Holmes," I burst out a little later, "it's not as if I possess your mind, you know? What is it you advise me to do?"

He pondered the question. "Perhaps what you need, Watson, is to embark upon an affair?"

I goggled at my friend. "An affair?" I choked. "Be gad, an

affair… At the age of fifty-five?"

Holmes raised an amused eyebrow. "Why not? Just last week Lady Allbrighton was enquiring as to your availability."

"Lady Allbrighton?"

"She has a friend, a widower in her early fifties."

"Are you playing matchmaker here, Holmes?"

He regarded the crime pages of the *London Gazette*. "Perish the thought."

"Anyway," I blustered, "I'm way past anything like that."

I was saved further embarrassment by a commotion in the street. Glancing through the window, I saw an automobile swerve to avoid an obstruction in the road, blaring its horn as it did so. The saloon had fetched up on the pavement and a noisy crowd had gathered and was remonstrating – not at the driver of the car, I hasten to add, but at the cause of the vehicle's sudden veering from the highway.

"My word," I gasped.

Planted in the very centre of the road, as solid and immovable as the trunk of an ancient oak, was the leading stanchion of a Martian tripod. The second and third legs – gun-metal grey girders pocked with rivets the size of saucers – were positioned respectively fifty yards away in the cobbled forecourt of the local brewery, and equidistant in the rose garden of Sir Humphrey Melville, M.P. – there would be questions raised in the House, no doubt.

Holmes, alerted by the commotion and the sudden eclipsing of the sunlight by the louring metal cowl high above, joined me at the window.

We stared up in time to see a hatch in the curved underbelly of the tripod swing open like a bomb-bay door: what emerged from within, however, was not a projectile but the squat, tentacled form – hideous in the extreme – of a Martian.

As we watched, the alien descended on an elevator plate, its progress observed by a growing crowd. For all that our overlords' many vehicles and ironclads dominated the landscape of our towns and cities, the Martians themselves were rarely seen in the flesh; therefore the descent of this ugly specimen to street level caused something of a stir amongst the observers.

A police constable was soon on the scene, and this worthy met the Martian at ground level and escorted the creature through the rapidly parting crowd.

"I do believe," I said, "that the Martian is heading in this direction."

"Indeed," said Holmes, rubbing his hands, "and that can mean only one thing: that the Martians once again require my assistance."

The alien passed beneath our window and approached the front door. Two minutes later Mrs Hudson entered the room, somewhat flustered.

"Oh, Mr Holmes! I know I shouldn't say this, what with these 'ere creatures running things as they are, and knowing how you hob-nob with them from time to time... but there's another of the slimy things downstairs – well, on its way up, right now. It gave its name, but for the life of me I couldn't make sense of its burblings."

"It will be none other than Gruvlax-Xenxa-Schmee, I shouldn't wonder. Be so kind as to show him in, Mrs Hudson, and if you would prepare a pot of Earl Grey..."

She bustled out, and in due course the door opened and the Martian squeezed his bulk through the narrow door-frame and shuffled into the room.

Holmes advanced and shook one of the creature's tentacles. He bowed, murmured a greeting in the Martian's own gargling tongue, then continued in English, "Gruvlax-Xenxa-Schmee, I am delighted to welcome you again to 221B. You have of course met my good friend, Dr Watson."

I essayed a nod in the alien's direction, loath to match Holmes' greeting and grip the slimy tentacle. I hoped the creature would not be offended at this perceived breech of etiquette. Gruvlax-Xenxa-Schmee was the deputy ambassador to Great

Britain, and a Very Important Alien.

He was squat, with a compact, cockroach-coloured torso set upon half a dozen thick legs or tentacles. He had no head as such: his facial features – a quivering, v-shaped beak and two huge cloudy eyes – were embedded in the scaly hide of his torso.

Added to the creature's unsightly appearance was his peculiar body odour: the sweet stench of putrid meat.

"Mrs Hudson is preparing the Earl Grey," Holmes said, "to which I recall you are rather partial. Please, take a seat."

The alien backed on to the *chaise longue*, the only piece of furniture in the room able to contain his broad bulk, and sat down. His beak rattled like a castanet and a burbling approximation of our language filled the air.

"It is my honour, good sirs, to make your esteemed acquaintance once again," he said. "Many months have passed since our last meeting, in which I have reflected happily upon the fine services you rendered to our embassy."

"All in the line of duty," Holmes said, pulling up a dining chair and seating himself before the alien. I remained at the table, watching the pair.

Almost a year ago the Martian Ambassador to Great Britain had been brutally murdered: an internal investigation by the Martians themselves had proved fruitless, and as a last resort the services of my friend were called upon. The case had taxed his considerable powers of deduction, but within days he had brought the culprit to book and earned the undying gratitude of the Martian race.

Mrs Hudson entered, bearing a silver tray with a teapot and three china cups and saucers. She retreated, averting her gaze from our guest, and Holmes poured the tea.

"Now," he said, sitting back with the saucer perched upon the prominence of his right knee, "how might I be of service?"

Before replying, the alien attended to his refreshment. Gripping the delicate china cup in one of his proboscis-like tentacles, the creature raised it to his beak and, rather than taking a small sip, tipped the entire contents of the cup into his maw. He made a gurgling sound, as if in appreciation, and Holmes refilled his cup.

"The matter is one of utmost delicacy," said Gruvlax-Xenxa-Schmee. "We cannot allow the news to be disseminated abroad, for fear of causing fear and consternation."

Holmes nodded. "And the nature of the crime?"

"The gravest, the very gravest, my friend. Murder."

"I see..." Holmes said, leaning forward, "and the victim of the crime?"

"None other than the esteemed philosopher Delph-Smanx-Arapna," said Gruvlax-Xenxa-Schmee.

I looked at Holmes. The name meant nothing to me, but then I took very little interest in the high and mighty amongst the ranks of our alien overlords. By the frown that creased my friend's aquiline features, I gathered that the name was taxing his powers of recall, too.

"Delph-Smanx-Arapna was one of our finest thinkers," the Martian went on, "belonging to the Zyrna-Ximon school of thought. He was also a Venerable; that is, a Master entering his one hundredth Martian year, which approximates to one hundred and ninety Earth years."

"Venerable indeed," Holmes assented. "And do you, or rather the Martian authorities, have any clue as to who might have wanted the Venerable dead?"

The alien poured the second cup of Earl Grey into his mouth, gurgled his appreciation, then said, "Delph-Smanx-Arapna's views were seen, among certain sections of Martian society, as contentious. But as to why anyone might disagree with his ideas to the point of wishing his death..." He lifted three tentacles in an evident gesture of mystification.

"How was Delph-Smanx-Arapna murdered?" Holmes asked.

"In the most despicable manner imaginable," came the reply. "His second forward tentacle was severed and then..." The v-shaped beak ceased its movement, and for a brief few seconds

Gruvlax-Xenxa-Schmee closed his huge, glaucous grey eyes. The alien was clearly moved by his recall of the murder. "And then the severed limb was utilised to block the philosopher's oesophagus. He died in terrible agony."

Holmes murmured his condolences. "I have read somewhere – I cannot recall where – that such a killing…"

The alien interrupted, "Just so. The killing in the manner I have described is known amongst my kind as *lykerchia*… It means, in English, 'to kill someone for the views they hold'… Such heinous murder is, thankfully, rare amongst our kind, which is why this particular crime is considered so revolting – and why not one word of it must filter out to the citizenry of my planet. The authorities have covered up his murder with the story that Delph-Smanx-Arapna passed away peacefully in his sleep."

"And might I enquire where the murder took place?" Holmes asked.

"He was murdered in his home, in Keshera. That is, in the Verdant Summerlands situated in the foothills of Olympus Mons."

"I see," said my friend, leaning back in his chair and stroking his chin. "Now, I take it that you have reason to believe that the perpetrator of this dastardly crime has fled to Earth, hence your request for my assistance in the matter?"

"We are confident that the killers are still on Mars," the alien replied. "It would be impossible for them to have left our planet, as flights to Earth are strictly monitored. Only accredited politicians, the military, and selected artists and musicians are accorded transit passes to your world."

Holmes tapped his chin and stared into space for a while. Then he fixed the alien with a gaze and asked, "And so you wish me to conduct an investigation into the murder of Delph-Smanx-Arapna at a remove of some… sixty million miles?"

The Martian lofted two tentacles in a gesture known only to himself. "On the contrary, Mr Holmes. We are desirous of your presence *in situ*, so that you might better conduct your investigations. I am here to invite you, and your esteemed friend Dr Watson, to journey to Mars as our honoured guests."

The alien's words rendered me, for the time being, speechless; likewise Holmes, but not for long. "That is a most gracious honour indeed," said he. "And one which I must discuss with Dr Watson. I trust that you do not require an immediate decision? There are various details that require our attention; arrangements to be made and appointments postponed..."

The alien waved a tentacle. "I fully understand," he said, "but I must stress that time is of the essence. A liner leaves the Batteresea docking station at two tomorrow afternoon. Another ship does not leave, after that, for a month. We would require your decision by six this evening, my friend. Needless to say, upon the successful outcome of the case, my government would ensure that you would be generously remunerated."

Holmes waved this aside. "Please, let us not sully the offer at this juncture with talk of monetary gain. I will require a few hours to discuss the matter with Dr Watson, and then, in the morning, if I agree to take on the case, I should like to further question yourself, and any of your colleagues you think might aid my investigations."

Gruvlax-Xenxa-Schmee rose to his six tentacles and looked from me to Holmes. "I await your decision with anticipation," he said. "For now, farewell."

The alien lumbered from the room and I turned to my friend. "Well, Holmes..." I said in great excitement. "We're going, of course? We can't really look such a gift horse in the mouth, can we?"

A look of abstraction passed across my friend's ascetic features. "On the face of it, you're right, Watson. How I have dreamed of one day setting foot upon the Red Planet! How I have mused about embroiling myself in their unique and mysterious culture! To think of it, Watson – to walk the red sands beneath the mustard skies of Mars... to look upon the Plane of Utopia from the slopes of Phlegra Montes!"

"I sense a but approaching, Holmes..."

"But, Watson, Gruvlax-Xenxa-Schmee's request puzzles me somewhat. Very well, I rendered the Martians a great service a year ago in finding the killer of their ambassador, but then the killing occurred on our doorstep, as it were, and to solicit my services then was the logical option. But to request that I investigate the killing of a Martian philosopher on his own planet, when the Martians' own detectives would be better suited to deal with the matter... It vexes me not a little, Watson."

"But what ulterior motive might they have?" I asked. "If indeed you suspect an ulterior motive?"

My friend shook his head. "That is just the problem. For the life of me, I don't know what I suspect, and this troubles me."

He paced the room, his chin sunk upon his chest, and perhaps five minutes later looked up and said, "I'm going to the British Library, Watson. There are one or two details I wish to check. It concerns me that, for all the comprehensiveness of the *Encyclopedia Martiannica*, nowhere does it mention the philosopher Delph-Smanx-Arapna. Now there is probably a valid reason for this, and if so then my doubts might very well be for nought. Inform Mrs Hudson that I will be back for dinner at six, would you?"

And, with this, Holmes flung his overcoat about his lank frame and hurried from the room.

Two
Conversation in the Park

I was in a state of febrile excitation and anticipation for the rest of the day. Unable to settle to *The Times* crossword, after lunch I took myself from the house and wandered the streets until finding myself at Hyde Park.

A Martian tripod stood sentinel beside Marble Arch, something grave and monumental in its very silence and stillness. For the most part these great ironclads, stationed at strategic locations about London, remained in situ; it was the smaller tripods – such as we had seen in Baker Street that morning, bearing Gruvlax-Xenxa-Schmee – that were ambulatory. The stationary behemoths such as the one here were the very vehicles that had wrought such havoc around the world a decade ago, until common terrestrial viruses had proved the invader's undoing. Little did we know back then, as we celebrated our unlikely salvation, that soon a second wave of Martian battleships would be on its way across the gulf of space, this armada bearing extraterrestrials inoculated against Earth's microscopic defenders.

Later this evening, as at every sunset since the second invasion, the sentinel tripods ranged around London would begin their signature call: "Ulla, ulla… Ulla, ulla…" The eerie double-note, plangent and melancholic, would eddy across the rooftops of the boroughs, as one tripod enigmatically called to another, just once, in an acoustic chain diminishing from west to east and, eventually, fading into the distance beyond Barnes.

I passed the tripod and continued to Speakers' Corner.

A protest or demonstration of some sort was in progress here, and I slowed my walk to take in the swelling crowd and the platform of speakers.

Five men and women stood upon the platform beneath a banner which declared: "Terra for the Terrans! Free Earth Now!" Amongst the crowd I espied home-made placards bearing such legends as: "Martians Go Home!" and "The Tyranny Must End!"

A tall, full-bearded figure in his fifties, I judged, stepped up to a microphone and began his peroration, and as I moved closer to the platform I realised that the speaker was none other than the celebrated playwright George Bernard Shaw. Seated beside him as he awaited his turn at the microphone, harrumphing through his moustache like some huge, disgruntled walrus, I recognised G. K. Chesterton: I smiled my amusement that it had taken the arrival of the Martians to bring these two literary giants, normally at polemical loggerheads, to some form of rapprochement.

"Domination of one race by another can never, ever, under any circumstances, be tolerated; look upon the sorry plight of those countries and peoples under the oppression of our very own Empire. Ask the citizens of India and Africa if they welcome our rule, depriving them as it does of the opportunity to grow as nations, to express their sovereign individuality. I say that the same is true now, on Earth, as humankind grovels under the tyrannical heel of our otherworldly oppressors!"

Cheers greeted Shaw's words, as he went on to enumerate his grievances in more specific terms. I estimated the crowd now numbered a couple of hundred, made up of citizens from all walks of society; barrow-boys and costermongers rubbed shoulders with bowler-hatted bankers and businessmen in pin-stripes. I made out dowagers and dustbin men, aristocrats and artisans; if nothing else, opposition to the Martian's occupation had produced a democratising effect amongst the populace.

Though it struck me that, perhaps, just as many people, and from just as broad a cross-section of society, saw the benefits that the Martians had brought to our world.

I was casting my glance about the crowd when I caught the eye of a rather striking young woman standing at my side.

She was attired in a jade green ankle-length dress, with a lace cloche perched on her head at a jaunty angle. Her hair was golden blonde, her face pale and breathtakingly beautiful, with a symmetry of feature set off by a wide, smiling mouth whose full lips suggested to me a happy and generous nature.

She noticed my attention and smiled. "Mr Shaw performs his usual trick of revealing truths with uncommon insight, don't you think?"

I smiled to myself: the young woman possessed intelligence to complement her beauty.

I ventured, "That all depends, I suppose, on whether you consider the Martian's presence good or ill."

She looked at me. "Are you here to join the protest, Mr...?"

I offered my hand. "Doctor," I said. "Doctor John Watson, at your service. And you might be?"

She blessed me with a delightful smile and took my hand. "Freya Hadfield-Bell."

"And you are here because you side with Shaw, Chesterton and the rest?" I enquired.

She raised a finger. "But I asked you first, Dr Watson..."

I laughed, "So you did! Very well... I am here through happenstance, as I was taking an afternoon constitutional. And as to whether I oppose the presence of the Martians... I must admit that I can see both benefits and disadvantages." A thought occurred to me, and I indicated the café beside the Serpentine that served afternoon teas. "I wonder if you would care to join me in refreshment, Miss Hadfield-Bell?"

"Do you know, I rather think I would, Doctor."

"Capital!" I said, and led the way to the café.

We took our seats and I ordered tea and cakes, Darjeeling for my attractive companion and Earl Grey for myself.

"Now," she said as she raised the china cup to her lips, and took a tiny sip, "those benefits you mentioned, Dr Watson?"

"It cannot be denied," I began, "that the coming of the Martians has revolutionised our understanding of the sciences, and the benefits accruing from this are indisputable..."

She pointed an elegant forefinger at me; she was, for a woman of tender years, rather forthright, and I found this somewhat refreshing. "But who gains from this 'revolution', Doctor? Do you realise that the profits made from the increase in manufacturing goes not into the coffers of our government, but straight back to our oppressors on Mars? Do you realise too that poverty in this country, in real terms, has increased for the majority since the Martian invasion? Oh, the Martians might condescend to give us advanced medicines and Electrical Automobiles and other meretricious gewgaws to keep the populace subdued, but without doubt the Martians are stripping our planet of resources for their own material gain."

I smiled to myself. "Now I understand your presence here, Miss Hadfield-Bell. You clearly oppose Martian rule."

"I shock you, Dr Watson?"

"Not at all. I am rather impressed by your arguments, and the manner in which you express yourself. The term 'a breath of fresh air' comes to mind. From one so young and..." I faltered.

She frowned. "I detect a patronising note in your assessment, Dr Watson. My age and gender, I rather think, do not enter into the equation." She gestured to the crowd and the speakers. "Minds greater than mine can see the iniquity of the Martian regime. But it does not take intelligence or insight to realise that the arrival of the Martians is founded on a great and terrible lie..." At this she bit her lip, and it occurred to me that she had vouchsafed more than she thought safe to let slip.

"I am intrigued," said I. "Please, go on..."

She took a breath in hesitation, regarding her half-finished Darjeeling. At last she said, "The Martians would have us believe that the first wave of invaders from the Red Planet were of a tyrannical political faction that had gained dominance on Mars through ruthless oppression of the populace, terrible wars, and merciless pogroms; the invasion of Earth, current Martian leaders maintain, was but the logical consequence of that bellicose regime: they had subdued their own world and, seeking others to oppress, and more valuable territory to occupy, had set their eyes on Earth. The story goes – or so our Martian overlords would like us to believe – that these initial aggressors were brought to their knees by the common terrestrial virus… and that the second wave of Martians comprised of the more peaceable, liberal schism left behind on Mars. They further assure us that the two are distinct, and that our current Martian oppressors bear no relation to the former tyrants."

I sat back, hiding a smile of amusement at her fervour. It made her even more beautiful, I thought. "And you think differently, Miss Hadfield-Bell?"

She swept on, "They would have us believe that, with the invasion forces intent on the subjugation of Earth, defences back on Mars were neglected, and that the liberal forces then took advantage to wrest control of the scant armies left behind. They say that they despatched a liner to Earth, and that a scientific team alighted in Africa and manufactured an antidote to the virus that had put paid to the initial invasion."

"And according to you?"

She smiled, but without an iota of humour. She fixed me with a steely gaze. "The fact is, Dr Watson, that the Martians, the initial wave and the second front, are one and the same. It was merely a political expedient, promulgated by the second set of invaders, to claim that the original were murderous tyrants. Oh, they worked it very cleverly; I would go so far as to say that they were politically brilliant – and we, sad dupes that we were, played into their hands and fell for their lies hook, line and sinker."

"You seem," I said, "certain of your rather… lurid accusations."

She smiled at me frostily. "I am as certain as I can be," she said.

"And how is that?"

She hesitated. "I would rather, at this juncture, keep my sources to myself."

"Very well..." I said, and sipped my tea. "But look here, if you were right, then surely we would have heard a rumour of it by now? The papers would be full of..."

"The papers," she almost spat, "are controlled by the Martians. The press barons are in cahoots with the ruling Martian elite. They print lurid accounts of life on Mars, shallow travelogues to amuse the masses, and trumpet the benefits the invasion has brought, and all the while the barons and the editors are mere patsies to our oppressors, raking in their millions with lies and untruths."

I sat forward. "You intrigue me. I hear what you say, but, without corroboration to back up your claims..."

"Without corroboration, Dr Watson, you think my stories the mere flights of fancy of an impressionable young woman?"

"Why, I think nothing of the kind!" I expostulated.

"But your entire manner, if I might make so bold, has been rather superior throughout our meeting. You have the air of someone allowing a child to chatter loquaciously, while you sit content in the assumption of your own superiority. Oh, I've seen your type before. What we need, once we've got rid of the egregious Martians, is another revolution to sweep away old, conservative values and traditional ideas!"

"I take it, Miss, that you are a suffragette?"

She glared at me and, I rather think, blasphemed under her breath, "*Good God!*"

She hurriedly gathered her bag and made to depart.

I reached out so as to delay her precipitate departure. "I wonder if we might meet again..." I said.

She snatched her hand away, said, "That, Dr Watson, remains to be seen," and swept – rather regally, I thought – away.

I sat in silence for a while, digesting her words and feeling both chastised and, oddly, invigorated by the meeting with such a feisty young woman.

In due course I finished my tea and retraced my steps back to Baker Street.

Three
The Mystery Deepens

I found my friend deep in a brown study when I returned; he was pacing back and forth, chin sunk upon his chest and his fists thrust into the pockets of his dressing gown. He hardly acknowledged my arrival, merely grunted at my greeting, and I knew better than to derail his train of thought.

Over dinner he emerged from his reverie, and I felt emboldened enough to enquire: "Well, Holmes, did you learn anything at the British Library?"

"The mystery deepens, Watson."

"How so?"

"I asked to see certain obscure Martian texts upon my arrival at the library," he said. "They were not the originals, of course, but rather translations. They pertained to somewhat abstruse areas of Martian philosophy – you see, I was certain that in these tomes I would find reference to the work, if not the life, of the philosopher Delph-Smanx-Arapna."

"Let me guess," I said, slicing into my pork chop: "there was no reference to be found, hm?"

"Your sagacity astounds me, Watson. You're right. There was no mention of the fellow. Likewise his name seemed to have been excised from more recent periodicals and journals. Although there was reference aplenty to other Martian thinkers, there was not a smidgen to be found on Delph-Smanx-Arapna."

"Perhaps," I surmised, "he just wasn't of the first rank–"

"Yet according to Gruvlax-Xenxa-Schmee," Holmes said, "he was feted as one of the finest Martian minds of the current era."

"So what the deuce do you think is going on?"

He pursed his thin lips thoughtfully. "That, my friend, we might very well find out when we set foot on the Red Planet."

"We're going!" I proclaimed.

"I contacted Gruvlax-Xenxa-Schmee as soon as I returned," he said. "Our berths are booked aboard the liner *Valorkian*, leaving Battersea docking station at two o'clock tomorrow. One week later we will be on Mars."

"My word..." I laughed. "You were not deterred by finding no mention of what's-his-name?"

Holmes smiled. "On the contrary, Watson, my curiosity was fired. It makes the puzzle all the more intriguing, does it not? Now the mystery is not only who might have ended the life of the Martian philosopher, but why has all mention of the worthy been omitted from every pertinent translation on Earth?"

"Of course, there might be a perfectly innocent explanation."

"You are right, there might be. I hope to learn more when I question Gruvlax-Xenxa-Schmee and his colleagues at the Martian embassy in the morning. I have been granted an appointment at ten, for one hour. I would be grateful, Watson, if you could pack a chest with a few of my belongings while I'm away in the morning, and then take a cab to Battersea, meeting me there at noon. Oh, and I think that it might be wise if I took along my Webley."

"You expect trouble?"

"One must prepare for every eventuality," said my friend.

Mrs Hudson entered the room, cleared away the dishes, and asked if we wanted coffee; Holmes requested Turkish, and I joined him in a cup.

A while later, as we sat on either side of the hearth, nursing out coffee cups, Holmes said, "And how went your day, Watson?

I see that you took a stroll around Hyde Park, listened to the speakers demonstrating against the Martian presence and, if I am not mistaken, took tea with a rather fetching member of the opposite sex."

I lowered my cup and stared at my friend in vexed admiration. "Confound it, Holmes! How can you possibly know?"

"Simplicity itself, my dear Watson. You returned with a copy of the *Weekly Sketch*, a periodical you purchase only when you take a turn around the Serpentine; that you paused to listen to the speakers at Hyde Park corner is a given, as I read the notice advertising the demonstration in yesterday's *Times*, and I have observed your enjoyment of public debate."

"Very well," I said, "but how can you possibly know that I met a rather charming young filly?"

Holmes cracked a smile. "Watson, old man, I can read you like a book: the light in your eyes, your somewhat dreamy abstraction, that witless smile that crosses your face from time to time when you consider the meeting. I have seen it again and again, over the years."

"Witless...?" I muttered.

"And if that were not enough, then the Earl Grey tea leaves adorning your waistcoat, adhering there from a spillage, I surmise, indicate that you paused for refreshment – and, as you rarely do so alone, it is evident that you were accompanied."

"You're absolutely right, Holmes. As a matter of fact I did meet a rather remarkable young woman."

"I am amazed that you should with such celerity take up my suggestion of this morning," he said with a half-smile, "and endeavour to embark upon an affair."

I feared I coloured somewhat as I replied, "Oh, it was nothing like that, old boy."

"I rather think you protest too much, Watson. I think you're smitten. "

"No, not in the least. Perish the thought!" I blustered. "Admittedly she was a corker, I'll give you that, but her ideas were somewhat farfetched, to say the least."

"Farfetched?"

I outlined my conversation with Miss Freya Hadfield-Bell, and her opinion that our current Martian overlords were one and the same with the original murderous mob.

"The notion is absurd," I said. "I can't begin to imagine how she got it into her pretty young head."

Holmes regarded the dregs of his coffee, then said, "I have heard the theory mooted in learned circles on more than one occasion, Watson. Mark my word, there might be a grain of truth in the idea."

I goggled at him. "You really think so, Holmes?"

He set his cup aside. "Shaw and Chesterton are convinced that such is the case," said he. "Just the other week G.K. bent my ear on the very subject at the Athenaeum. I remained ambivalent. Perhaps, my friend, we might learn more on this matter, and others, when we set foot on the sands of Mars one week from the morrow, hm?"

"Indeed we might, Holmes," said I, and a little later we retired to our rooms.

His words set me to thinking, and that night I lay awake long into the early hours before sleep finally came.

Four
All Aboard for the Red Planet!

The Martian docking station at Battersea is one of the wonders of the world.

As one approaches from across the Thames, the station dominates the skyline of south London, a series of jet black gantries, towers and the bulbous, geodesic domes – the latter a peculiarity of Martian architecture, I understand – which resemble nothing so much as gross carbuncles. Covering an area of three miles by two, the station consists of half a dozen docking rings, where interplanetary ships make their landfall, and as many mobile gantries, great girder frameworks on an extensive network of rails.

The station is a hive of industry, with a constant toing and froing of all manner of transportation; there is even a dedicated railway station to ferry passengers and goods from the newly arrived ships to the centre of London. A veritable small town of commerce has grown up around the port, with crowds of human servitors bustling hither and thither. Glimpsed in amongst, from time to time, one can observe the form of vehicle preferred by the Martians when not riding their iconic tripods: these are bulky, domed cars like trilobites, which beetle busily back and forth on three wheels.

At noon precisely I stepped from my cab, found a porter, and had him transport our cases through the busy concourse of the station to the vast, glass-covered disembarkation lounge. This resonant chamber was occupied, for the most part, by tentacled Martians – no doubt diplomats, traders and the like, come to the end of their secondment on planet Earth: I wondered if they were longing for the red sands of their homeplanet after their sojourn on our strange world.

A dozen or so humans stood among the alien crowd, with chests and cases at their feet. These I took to be businessmen and civil servants; one fellow – a singular specimen of humanity, perhaps only a little over five feet high but as broad across the shoulders as a bull – struck me as familiar. I was sure I had seen his barrel chest, great head, and flowing black beard pictured in some periodical. He wore a tropical suit as if equipped for exploration, finished off with a solar topee.

I scanned the crowd, but of my friend there was no sign.

Through the glass roof of the chamber I made out the gargantuan shape of a Martian liner, its graphite-hued carapace pitted and excoriated with its passage through the void of space. Although it towered to a height of a hundred yards, yet it gave the impression of being squat, for it was perhaps thirty yards wide, its appearance made even broader by the addition of two scimitar-like tail-fins which flared from its base. This, evidently, was the *Valorkian*, the vessel which would transport Holmes and me to the Red Planet.

I had done a little preliminary reading on the subject of interplanetary travel, and learned that we would pass the bulk of the week-long journey under sedation, with only a few hours at take-off and landing being spent fully conscious. This was perhaps just as well, for a week's confinement in a small cabin was the definition of tedium. At least we would be able to look out upon our world as it diminished in our wake – and view our destination when we approached the orb of Mars.

I was day-dreaming of our arrival there, and what adventures might await us, when I was hailed by a familiar voice and I turned to see Sherlock Holmes approaching, accompanied by a squat Martian scurrying along on his six ambulatory tentacles.

"All set, Watson?" my friend enquired.

"Everything packed, as you instructed, Holmes," said I, indicating our cases and giving Holmes a wink to inform him that I had not forgotten to pack his firearm.

Holmes gestured to the Martian at his side. "Gruvlax-Xenxa-Schmee," he said, "will be making the journey too; he will be our guide while on the Red Planet."

"Capital," I said, nodding at the alien.

"It will be my honour to show you around our capital city, my friends, before your investigations commence."

"Most kind of you," I murmured.

"Now, if you will excuse me for a moment, I must ensure that all the relevant details are in order..." and so saying he scurried off towards a counter behind which stood a human custom's official.

"Well, Holmes," I said when we were alone, "what did you learn?"

"Precious little," he said. "I informed Gruvlax-Xenxa-Schmee about the curious absence of all mention of the philosopher from the relevant literature, but he waved it away as of no concern. According to him, only a fraction of all information regarding the Red Planet is translated. There is hardly the time to render all information into English – or, he added, the need. For who, after all, would be interested in many of the more arcane aspects of Martian life?"

"And what did you make of this reason?" I asked.

"Specious in the extreme, Watson. I know that the finest minds of Earth are eager to learn everything possible about Mars, its history, culture and philosophies... and the idea that all mention of one of its finest thinkers should be denied to mankind... No, Watson, I find the entire business decidedly rum."

Before I could question my friend as to his notions why the

Martians should have elided mention of the philosopher from all Earthly literature, a stentorian boom all but deafened me.

"Holmes, be Gad! As I live and breathe, what the deuce are you doing here?"

I turned to see the huge man I had noticed earlier bearing down upon us like a charging bull.

Holmes turned and, beholding our interlocutor, a smile cracked his visage. "Challenger! What a sight for sore eyes! You look set for an adventure into darkest Africa, sir."

The great man bellowed his mirth. "Africa? Perish the thought! I've charted that neck of the woods, old boy. Now I'm set for pastures new."

"Mars, I presume?"

"None other." He gestured through the glass roof at the *Valorkian*. "Leaving aboard that ugly old can on the dot of two. And you?"

"Likewise," said Holmes.

"Capital! We should take tea – or whatever noxious beverage the Martian might serve – on our arrival."

Holmes introduced us. "Watson, meet my old friend, Professor George Edward Challenger, zoologist, explorer, and adventure extraordinaire. Challenger, my friend and faithful companion, Dr John Watson."

The professor gripped my hand. I winced. "Delighted," I said, retrieving my hand and massaging life back into the crushed metacarpal.

"But what takes you to the Red Planet?" Holmes asked.

"A spot of lecturing, followed by a bit of sight-seeing. The Martians are more than eager to avail themselves of my expertise in the area of Terran fauna, don't y'know? I hope to climb Olympus Mons, if my hosts are willing, and I have a mind to sail the southern seas. I'd like to bag the mammoth leviathan said to haunt those waters, but getting the trophy home might prove somewhat problematical, what? But you? What takes you to Mars?"

I glanced at my friend, who said, "The Martians have roped me in to do a little investigating – but more of that later," he hurried on as he beheld the return of Gruvlax-Xenxa-Schmee.

The professor tapped the side of his nose. "Understood, Holmes. We should shoot the breeze beneath the light of Phobos! Excuse me while I ensure my crates are properly stowed." And so saying he hurried across the concourse to where a porter was labouring with three vast timber chests.

"Everything is in order, gentlemen," the Martian said. "We should proceed to the check-in desk."

We passed through a perfunctory customs check, then across the apron of the station towards the bulk of the waiting ship. Seen at close quarters, I was struck by the craft's size and latent power – and by its bizarre alien quality. This was a vessel constructed by an alien race, and therefore like nothing made by mankind. Its carapace was dark and bulbous, and somehow appeared almost *biological*, like the epidermis of some great ocean-dwelling leviathan.

We stepped into its shadow, climbed on to a commodious elevator plate, and were whisked in seconds into the craft's arching atrium. Martians and humans alike scurried back and forth; I noticed, among the crowd, a dozen or so green-uniformed men and women who were employed as pursers and stewards by the shipping line.

Gruvlax-Xenxa-Schmee led the way to another elevator plate, and this one lofted us to a gallery that ran around equatorial circumference of the ship. We proceeded along a narrow curving passageway until we came to a series of rectilinear portholes set in the outer skin. Straps hung to either side of these viewing portals, and our Martian guide advised that we should take a firm grip on these when the ship took off.

In due course a thunderous rumble shook the vessel, and motion like an earthquake almost knocked me from my feet. "Whoa!" I cried, and not a second too soon gripped the straps. The ferocious roar increased. I pressed my nose to the glass and beheld, in wonder, the grid-like streets of London pull ever so slowly away… Never before had I flown – not trusting the new-fangled, flimsy aeroplanes with my life – but the sensation I experienced now was not what I might have expected flight to be: rather, it was like being carried into the heavens by some vast, slow-moving elevator. As I stared out, all London became visible beneath me, and I spotted familiar landmarks down below like architect's scale models: there was Buckingham Palace, and here St. Paul's; tiny Electrical Automobiles whizzed back and forth, and citizens crowded the thoroughfares of the Strand and Pall Mall, overlooked here and there by Martian tripods.

Soon all detail was lost to sight, other than the pattern of the capital's streets, shot through by the great squiggle of the Thames. Fifteen minutes later we were at such an elevation that the coastline came into view, the bright blue of the channel contrasting with the verdant pastures and orchards of Kent.

In due course, as we sailed into the heavens high above Europe, Gruvlax-Xenxa-Schmee suggested that he show us to our berths. These were small cabins, barely larger than water-closets, and each contained a metal pod suggestive of a futuristic coffin. Our alien guide explained that we should undress, stow our clothing in the locker provided, and climb into the 'suspension pod', as he called it. He counselled us not to be alarmed when we were submerged, up to our neck, in an enveloping gel which would take care of our every bodily function for the duration of the voyage. Presently a human steward would come along to administer the sedative.

The Martian departed, taking Holmes to his own cabin, and I closed the outer door and regarded the 'suspension pod' with some scepticism. Taking a breath, I undressed, lifted the lid of the pod, and stepped gingerly into its confines. The pod was canted at a thirty-five degree angle, with at its upper end a wooden support for one's neck and head. No sooner had I settled myself in its length, and pulled down the door which covered my body but left my head free, than I felt the insidious tickle of some viscous fluid rise around my legs and torso. Cold at first, the fluid gel soon warmed up, and the sensation, as it submerged me to the neck, was not unpleasant.

An alarm pinged, no doubt alerting a steward to my readiness, and seconds later a unformed young woman entered the cubicle bearing a small cup.

"Now drink this straight down, Dr Watson, and the next thing you know you'll be waking up high above Mars."

I hardly heard her words, for I was staring in amazement at the young woman's singular beauty.

"But..." I said as the sedative took effect, a dozen questions on my lips.

For the steward was none other than Freya Hadfield-Bell...

Five
A Most Curious Note

Her last words were prescient: it seemed that no sooner had my eyes fluttered shut than I was struggling feebly awake, the gel draining from the pod. As I sat up and lifted the lid, I found it incredible to believe that a full seven days had elapsed. We were now sixty million miles from Earth, in orbit around the Red Planet.

These thoughts were pushed aside by the vision that entered my head of Freya Hadfield-Bell, followed by a slew of questions. Had our 'meeting' in Hyde Park been as accidental as it had seemed at the time? What was Hadfield-Bell, a self-confessed opponent of the Martian presence on Earth, doing here, working for the very Martians she considered her enemy? Had she manufactured our second meeting here aboard the *Valorkian*, and if so... why?

The alarm bell pinged, and I hurried to the locker and dressed quickly lest the young woman enter and find me *dishabille*.

I need not have worried, however, for when a tapping sounded at the door, it was not Hadfield-Bell but our alien guide.

"If you are quite ready, Doctor, would you care to join us as we come in to land?"

"I'll be with you in a jiffy," I said as I finished dressing. In due course I adjusted my collar and joined the alien in the corridor.

As we took an elevator plate down to the observation gallery, I said, "I was surprised to find that you employ human stewards aboard your ships."

"For the convenience of our human passengers," said Gruvlax-Xenxa-Schmee.

"And are these human employees resident on Mars?"

"For brief periods only," the alien replied. "They have what is known as a 'stopover', until they board the next returning ship for Earth."

The elevator plate reached its destination, and with an out-thrust tentacle my guide indicated that I should alight before him. I found Holmes a little further along the curving gallery, and beside him stood Professor Challenger. They were gripping the leather straps to either side of the portholes and staring out, Challenger bellowing his appreciation of the view.

I grasped the straps of the porthole next to Holmes, while Gruvlax-Xenxa-Schmee positioned himself beyond the professor.

"Developments!" I hissed at Holmes as I stared through the glass. We were sailing, as serene as any child's balloon, high above a rust-coloured desert, with wind-sculpted dunes running off towards the horizon like some fabulous alien script. Here and there far below I made out what I thought were great silver lakes – though time and experience were to put me right on that score – and die-straight canals that carried precious water from the poles to the equatorial regions.

"This is astounding!" Challenger bellowed like the bull he so resembled. "Why, look up to your right, Holmes! Now is that great tumbling spud Phobos or Deimos?"

"The former, Professor. Deimos, which is smaller, you will observe in the heavens to our left."

To me he whispered, "What is it, Watson?"

I peered along the corridor to ensure that Gruvlax-Xenxa-Schmee was out of earshot: the Martian seemed absorbed in the view of his homeworld. I said, "Freya Hadfield-Bell, the young woman I met in Hyde Park last week, is aboard this ship, working as a stewardess!"

"Not only beautiful, if your description is to be believed, but enterprising." He cogitated for a time. "It would appear, upon reflection, that your meeting in Hyde Park was not as accidental as you assumed at the time."

"That had occurred to me," I said.

"Did she have time to speak to you?"

I shook my head. "No, other than to tell me to drink the sedative, and that soon I'd awake above Mars. But..."

"Go on."

"But it can't be just a coincidence, can it? I mean, if she did arrange our meeting in the park..."

"Then," Holmes interjected, "she must therefore have had the intelligence that we had been invited to Mars, and so ensured her presence aboard the *Valorkian* accordingly. My admiration for the girl increases by the second."

"But what can she want, Holmes?"

"That remains to be seen. We must be vigilant."

I told him about the human stewards enjoying stopovers before boarding the next scheduled ship to Earth, and Holmes digested this and said, "In that case we must ascertain when the next ship leaves for home, so that we know how long we have in which to expect word from the girl."

"You think she'll contact us, Holmes?"

"Indubitably," said he.

My heart skipped at the thought, my excitation caused not merely by the derring-do inherent in the situation.

"By Jove!" Professor Challenger ejaculated. "Just feast your eyes on that, my friends!"

I returned my attention to the scene outside the ship. Far below, situated between two rearing mountain ranges, was a wide red plain covered in a webwork of what looked like girders. On closer inspection, these girders proved to a be a vast network of rails – for upon them, or rather *depending* from them, I beheld carriages like bullets shooting back and forth. The web converged on an agglomeration of black, carbuncle-like domes, in the centre of which, like the bull's-eye at the centre of a dartboard, was a great docking station occupied by a dozen mammoth spaceships similar to the one carrying us to our destination.

"That," declared Holmes, "if I am not mistaken, is the city of Glench-Arkana, the capital of all Mars."

"And the greatest metropolis in the solar system," Gruvlax-Xenxa-Schmee informed us, "home to fifty million of my kind."

"Imagine," Challenger muttered. "Fifty million... That's more than the population of Great Britain – and all in one vast city!"

The ship decelerated, swung about and came in low over the metropolis. I stared down at great wide boulevards thronged with Martian pedestrians and trilobite vehicles, and lined with buildings that emerged from the ground at odd angles, like daggers thrust into the earth. Small air-cars, which the Martians had not introduced to Earth, buzzed about the sky like so many bluebottles. The effect was wholly novel and disconcertingly alien.

We approached the central docking station and came down slowly upon a great metal flange. The ship clanged like a struck bell and the roar of the engines diminished into silence.

"Welcome to Mars!" Gruvlax-Xenxa-Schmee declared. "Now if you would be so good as to follow me..."

We stepped aboard an elevator plate and descended to the arched atrium, where our fellow passengers, Martian and human, were gathered prior to disembarkation. I searched the crowd for the tall, blonde-haired figure of Freya Hadfield-Bell, but in vain, and surmised that the human crew of the *Valorkian* left the ship via a separate exit.

"You will find the gravity of my planet a little lighter than that of Earth," Gruvlax-Xenxa-Schmee explained. "Also, the oxygen content of our atmosphere is not as great as that to which you are accustomed. The effect will be similar to that which you might experience when dwelling at high altitude on your planet. I recommend you do not unduly exert yourselves, for fear of becoming somewhat light-headed."

Already the hatch of the ship was sliding open, admitting the planet's warm, oxygen-low atmosphere. I took a deep breath and was reminded of the rarefied air I had last breathed while serving my country in the Hindu Kush.

Some kind of flexible umbilical tunnel was manoeuvred up to the exit, and in due course we followed our guide from the ship.

"It is mid-afternoon at this longitude," Gruvlax-Xenxa-Schmee informed us. "I will take you to a hotel, where you can rest and refresh yourselves. For the rest of the day you will be free to wander our great city. At first light tomorrow, I will come for you in an air-car and I will show you a little of the city before we proceed north to the foothills of Olympus Mons, where our esteemed philosopher Delph-Smanx-Arapna made his home before his untimely demise."

We emerged from the umbilical into a great terminus, busy with scurrying Martians. The chamber was undecorated, the walls a uniform shade of taupe, and I was reminded rather of the rough adobe interior of a termite mound.

We retrieved our baggage, whereupon Gruvlax-Xenxa-Schmee escorted us from the building on to a metal deck from which domed air-cars arrived and departed like bumblebees at a hive.

At this juncture we took our leave of Professor Challenger, arranging to meet him at his hotel – the Smerzna'gharan – in two hours for drinks.

An air-car descended before us, and our guide gestured that we should climb into the rear.

As the vehicle took off, with Gruvlax-Xenxa-Schmee in the front passenger seat beside the driver, I stared down at the teeming boulevards of Glench-Arkana. Crowds thronged the thoroughfares, and I beheld what might have been a market-place far below, selling who knew what exotic commodities? A strange scent reached my nostrils, which I would forever associate with the atmosphere of the Red Planet – an odour of indefinable spices mixed with the acrid tang of hot, lathe-turned metal.

The air-car banked and approached a jet black ziggurat, a stark silhouette against the mustard-coloured sky, an edifice which turned out to by our hotel. The vehicle came down gently and we alighted.

Gruvlax-Xenxa-Schmee remained in the passenger seat and lifted a tentacle in farewell. "I will collect you here at first light," said he.

I reached into my pocket out of habit, in search of small change for the cab driver – but came instead upon a square of folded paper as the air-car powered up and flew off.

"Hello," I said. "What on earth…?"

I pulled out the paper, unfolded it, and stared in disbelief at what was written there.

"Well, Watson?" Holmes enquired, watching me.

Not a little startled, I read the note for a second time.

My Dear Dr Watson,

You and Mr Holmes are in extreme danger! Please follow the instructions set down here, and then destroy this note. You must meet me at the Percherian-Hutava eating house, along the side street to the north of your hotel, at sixteen o'clock this evening. You will undoubtedly be followed, but my comrades will ensure that this will be dealt with. You might not recognise me, therefore I will carry a green valise. When I have ensured that we are not observed, I will explain everything, and together we can decide what further action should be taken.

Yours faithfully,

Freya Hadfield-Bell.

Six

Rendezvous on the Red Planet

At half-past fifteen o'clock, we left the hotel and hurried through the bustling streets of Glench-Arkana. The short Martian day was drawing to a close, and beyond the horizon of domes and towers the sun was setting in a gorgeous laminate of lacquered oranges and pinks. We were the only humans abroad, and our passage down the alleys of the ancient city caused not a little commotion amongst the crowds. Martians turned and stared at us with their great grey plate eyes, and the air was filled with the twitter of their commentary. I glanced behind us once or twice, but if we were being followed, I saw no sign.

"But what on earth did she mean, Holmes, when she wrote that we might not recognise her? Of course we will – she's a rather striking specimen of womankind, mark my word. She'd stick out among the Martians like a veritable sore thumb."

"I rather think she was suggesting she would be in disguise," Holmes said.

"Disguise?" I laughed at this. "She would be hard pressed to disguise herself so that she wasn't obvious in a crowd of Martians!"

"We shall see," Holmes said, and indicated a narrow alley. "This way."

As planned, we were taking a circuitous route to the

Percherian-Hutava eating house, the better to give Hadfield-Bell's comrades an opportunity to delay anyone who might be following us. Holmes had studied a map of the area, and committed the route to his excellent memory. We passed down a thoroughfare given over to the sale of piled spices and exotic examples of fruit or vegetables; the narrow street was packed with Martian pedestrians and domed bubble-vehicles: it reminded me, in its hustle and hubbub, of a Kabul marketplace.

At one point we heard a screech of brakes and turned to witness, a hundred yards in our wake, an altercation between the driver of a three-wheeled bubble-car and a pedestrian. Holmes gripped my arm. "That is likely the work of Hadfield-Bell's comrades," said he. "Hurry – this way."

We darted down a narrow passageway, emerged in another busy thoroughfare, turned right and then crossed the street and dived down yet another alley. Holmes led the way at a brisk trot, and I followed, confident in my friend's sense of direction; by this time I was utterly lost.

Minutes later we came to a boulevard I thought I recognised: ahead was the stepped ziggurat of our hotel. Holmes ushered me down a side street and paused before an open-fronted restaurant above which was a legend in flowing Martian script.

"Here we are," said Holmes, consulting his time piece. "And just in time. I make it sixteen o'clock on the dot."

The eating area comprised a series of low metal tables surrounded not by chairs but by cushions; perhaps half the tables were occupied by seated Martians taking liquids from silver, fluted vessels and eating what looked like flaked fish from huge bowls. An aroma of spicy cooked meat filled the air. I scanned the restaurant, but of Freya Hadfield-Bell there was no sign.

Holmes led the way to a vacant table and we seated ourselves upon the floor, positioned with our backs to the wall the better to observe the entrance.

A Martian approached our table and spoke its gargling gobbledegook, to which Holmes replied in kind. The waiter scuttled away. "I ordered two hot spiced drinks which you will find not too dissimilar to Kashmiri tea," he informed me.

Another alien approached, and I assumed that this one would take our food order. I was about to tell Holmes that I had little appetite when I noticed that this Martian was carrying a small green valise.

I gripped my friend's arm and hissed, "The game is up, Holmes! Our friend has been rumbled – the brute has taken her green valise! Should we beat a hasty retreat?"

Holmes leaned forward and addressed the alien in its own language, to which the Martian replied and lowered itself to the cushions on the far side of the table.

"What did it say, Holmes?" I was frantic to know. "What has the accursed beast done to Hadfield-Bell?"

"Lower your voice," Holmes ordered. "You are attracting unnecessary attention."

"But, dash it all, man –!"

At this, the Martian reached a tentacle across the table and touched my hand.

"Don't be alarmed, Doctor," whispered the Martian in English. "It is I, Freya Hadfield-Bell, and this is a rubber Martian suit."

"What the...?"

I stared at the hideous headpiece of the alien, and, as I did so, its ugly beak opened to such an extent that I glimpsed within its mouth – and what I observed there caused me first to choke, and then to splutter with laughter.

Hadfield-Bell's uncommonly beautiful face grinned out at me, then gave a conspiratorial wink. The beak clacked shut, and she continued in lowered tones, "I am sorry if I alarmed you, but I was forced to don this disguise through direst necessity. It's dashed uncomfortable in here and hot into the bargain. I will be brief. My friends managed to waylay your tail, but the Martian authorities are so wily that they might have employed two or more agents to keep you under surveillance."

I said, "You said that you would explain everything..."

"And so I will," came her somewhat muffled reply.

She fell silent as our drinks arrived, and she ordered the same from the waiter.

When it had departed, Holmes said, "I take it, Miss Hadfield-Bell, that Watson and I were lured to Mars on false pretences?"

"Just so," she replied.

Holmes explained the spurious reason for our presence here. "My suspicion was aroused when I found no mention of a Martian philosopher, one Delph-Smanx-Arapna, in any periodical, encyclopaedia, or journal on Earth. It troubled me somewhat that my services should be sought by aliens who, undoubtedly, have their own excellent investigatory organs."

Her beverage arrived, and she waited until the waiter had scurried away before saying, "Like many a human before you, you have been brought here as part of the Martian's master-plan."

Holmes lowered his brow in a frown. "Which is?"

"No less than the total takeover of planet Earth and the eventual annihilation of the human race."

"Good God!" I exclaimed.

Holmes eyed the woman's disguise, deep in thought, then said, "If you don't mind my asking, Miss Hadfield-Bell, how did you become embroiled in opposition to the Martian government?"

I sipped my drink; its unusual spices danced across my tongue, ending with quite an alcoholic kick. I drained half the flute, then gave my full attention to the woman's hushed words.

"I applied to work as a steward on the Martian liners in a bid to see the solar system, in the spirit of adventure which has already taken me to all four corners of our own world. I craved far horizons, new experiences, and what could be more novel than to set foot upon the soil of an alien world? All was well for a few months: I did not suspect the Martians of being anything other than what they claimed: the altruistic second wave of explorers come to aid humankind with their superior science and technology."

"But what occurred to change your mind?" Holmes asked.

"I was approached, one leave period here in Glench-Arkana, by a Martian unlike any I had seen before – both in his physical appearance, and in his philosophy. This creature was shorter than the norm, his carapace a shade or two darker than the average Martian citizen of this latitude. This was soon explained. My interlocutor hailed not from equatorial Mars but from the far north, adjacent to the polar regions; he was of a different race from the specimens you see here. His people were considered primitive by the majority, and even intellectually backward, not unlike the opinion that prevails in Europe regarding Africans. He told me a terrible story of state repression, torture, and genocide – and I was later to see evidence to support his claims: moving pictorial images, showing the slaughter of innocents, the bombing of northern cities and towns. But this Martian had not waylaid me to complain of the injustice meted out to his fellows, but to warn me that this was but the start of the Martians' bellicosity."

"You mean...?" I began.

"The eventual wiping out of the human race," said she. "I witnessed enough to come over to the rebels' side, and fight for the cause of his people, along with hundreds of my fellow human beings."

"You mentioned that we were in danger," Holmes reminded her.

"Tomorrow at first light," she said, "you will be collected by Gruvlax-Xenxa-Schmee and taken across the city to the Institute of Martian Sciences. There you will undergo a process known as Cerebral Personality Scanning."

"What the...?" I muttered. "Cerebral Personality Scanning? What the deuce do you mean by that?"

Hadfield-Bell was about to reply, but at that second a small Martian advanced across the restaurant and paused beside our table. I sat back, fearing that the authorities were on to us, and had come to arrest our friend.

The alien leaned towards the rubber disguise containing Hadfield-Bell and spoke rapidly in a lowered tone. At its words, Hadfield-Bell struggled upright, manoeuvring her tentacles with obvious difficulty. She was assisted in this by the newcomer, who held out one of its forward tentacles to steady her.

"Your presence here has been reported to the authorities," she said. "An informant warns that security officials are on their way here as I speak. I must leave immediately. It is imperative that you inform Professor Challenger of what I have told you. He, too, is in danger. As I said, you will be taken across town in the morning and scanned: the process will not harm you, and the authorities will keep you alive but in custody, for the time being. I will do everything I can to secure your rescue, gentlemen, but now I must make haste."

And, so saying, she scurried from the restaurant with the newcomer and was soon lost to sight amidst the crowds in the street outside.

"Drink up, Watson," Holmes said, flinging a couple of notes upon the table. "We had better leave before the authorities arrive, so that we may alert Challenger to the situation."

I finished my drink, head swirling with the rush of alcohol, and followed my friend from the restaurant. Holmes turned right along the alley, came to a boulevard, and hailed a passing cab. He gave the driver – this worthy much agitated at the fact of its human fare – the name of Professor Challenger's hotel. Soon we were beetling at speed along the busy street, the driver turning its entire body to stare at us and subject Holmes to a barrage of questions.

In due course we alighted outside a hotel with an adobe exterior and slit windows. The professor himself was kicking his heels in the foyer, his bulk anomalous amidst the relatively small Martians. "Hell's teeth, Holmes! Where the blazes have y' been?"

"We were delayed," said my friend. "We need to speak, in private. There is a rooftop bar back at our hotel. I suggest we make our way there at once."

"Confound it, man, you're blabbing like the hero of a penny dreadful!"

But Holmes was already leading the way outside, and, harrumphing into his huge beard, the professor followed.

It was but a short walk through the busy streets to our hotel, and soon we were ensconced on cushions on the elevated rooftop with a spectacular view across the night-time city. A spangle of electric lights gave the aspect of a fun-fair, the spectacle matched by the spread of constellations high above.

As I searched the heavens for the bright star that would be Earth, Holmes gave the professor a résumé of what we had just learned from Hadfield-Bell.

Challenger listened in silence, his huge face growing ever redder with the passing seconds. As Holmes came to the end of his account, I thought that our friend was about to burst, or at least succumb to apoplexy.

"The fiends! The monstrous beasts! Y'know, I did wonder at me summons. I know I'm famous and all that, but why would a bunch of ugly Martians want to hear all about me travels in Arabia?" He stared from me to Holmes. "But what's all this about 'personality scanning' – and what the blue blazes do the critters want with us, if we've been lured here under false pretences?"

"That, my friend, we shall no doubt learn in time." Holmes turned to me. "You are quiet, Watson."

"Mmm. Just thinking about the young gal – I hope she knows what she's doing, Holmes. I'd hate it if she were to..."

"I wouldn't worry yourself on that score, my friend. From what I've seen of Miss Hadfield-Bell, she seems more than able to handle herself."

We sat in the clement evening and watched the last of the sunset, going over and over what we had learned, and counselling ourselves to vigilance. As we talked, bolstering our confidence with our shared humanity amidst so much that was eerily alien, I succeeded in locating the scintillating point of brightness that was planet Earth, and gained a measure of comfort from its presence.

It did not occur to me, not even for one second, that I might never again set foot on my homeworld.

Seven
Duplicity at the Scientific Institute

I spent a fitful night in my narrow hotel berth, on a short mattress meant for the truncated bodies of our hosts. I tossed and turned, my dreams full of hideous Martian visages, these nightmare masks interspersed with visions of Freya Hadfield-Bell's singular loveliness. In my dreams she was a prisoner of the Martians, stripped of her uniform and chained in a dungeon, awaiting the depredations of her evil tormentors.

I awoke at dawn to find my friend's mattress vacated; before I could bestir myself to worry for his safety, the hatch opened and Holmes ducked through, his arms laden with local fruit and a bottle of some refreshment.

"I thought it wise to purchase breakfast, as there is none to be had in the establishment and Gruvlax-Xenxa-Schmee did say that he would arrive for us at first light."

We sat on our bunks and ate the peculiar fruit – in shape resembling apples, but with a yeasty taste and the texture of soap. The liquid was pale green and milk-like; indeed, according to Holmes, it was the product of the Martian equivalent of the terrestrial cow, with a spicy taint that made me wince.

"Do you think it wise to go along with Gruvlax-Xenxa-Schmee?" I said at one point.

Holmes ruminated. "Not to do so, Watson, would alert him

to the fact that we know something is awry."

"I could always claim illness," I said, and indicated the soapy fruit. "You could say I've come down with food poisoning."

"I am curious to behold this Martian Institute of Science, and what it contains. Also, my curiosity is aroused by the girl's mention of the scanning process. What might the Martians be up to, Watson? Hadfield-Bell said that they would not harm us – quite yet..."

"And all this talk of the annihilation of the human race, Holmes... Do you think the girl was exaggerating?"

"Her claims are extreme indeed, Watson. But, if she does rescue us, as she promised, then I have no doubt that she will be eager to substantiate her dire warnings with hard evidence."

We finished our singular breakfast, then descended to the forecourt to await the arrival of Gruvlax-Xenxa-Schmee.

No sooner had we had stepped outside than a bulky air-car descended and a hatch like the wing of an insect pivoted open and a Martian gestured from within.

In the capacious rear compartment of the vehicle, which was furnished with plushly upholstered benches like a Pullman carriage, sat Professor Challenger.

"Our first port of call," Gruvlax-Xenxa-Schmee announced as we squeezed in beside Challenger, "is the Martian Institute of Science. Professor Challenger's lecture is scheduled for this evening, and I thought he too might care to come along."

I exchanged a glance with Holmes, who said, "Capital idea, my friend. I am more than a little curious about the many wonders of your nigh miraculous technologies."

The air-car powered up with a roar of engines, and in a second we were airborne.

I watched the land slip away below us, my stomach turning at the thought of what might lie ahead. I recalled Hadfield-Bell's words, and gazed with new hostility at our hideous host and his driver. The Martians were, at the best of times, ugly in the extreme, with their cockroach-coloured tegument, their greasy bristles sprouting from the crater-like follicles that pitted their hides, and their great glaucous staring eyes. It had been some years, after the second wave of Martians arrived on Earth amid apologies for the behaviour of their more bellicose cousins, that mankind had been able to look upon the physicality of the extraterrestrials with anything like equanimity: it did not require much to cast them in the role, in my eyes at least, of the devils we had originally thought them to be.

Gruvlax-Xenxa-Schmee turned in his seat and eyed us. "I understand that you elected to take a stroll before dinner last night?"

"That's right," Holmes said. "We passed a pleasant hour or so taking in the market streets in the vicinity of the hotel."

"And you were not... troubled by the disturbance in that district?"

I glanced at my friend. Was Gruvlax-Xenxa-Schmee referring to the distraction that had resulted in our minders losing sight of us?

"We did notice a commotion at one point," Holmes said, "an altercation between the driver of a car and a pedestrian."

"There have been instances of terrorist activity in the area," said Gruvlax-Xenxa-Schmee.

"Terrorist activity?" Holmes raised an eyebrow.

Our guide waved a tentacle. "Hotheads from the northern deserts," he said, "demanding greater access to water or some such." He changed the subject. "I trust you found a suitable dining establishment during your sojourn?"

"A pleasant little restaurant not far from our hotel," said Holmes.

"And you were not pestered by importuning individuals eager to speak to human beings?"

"Ah..." Holmes temporised, "we did speak to one or two individuals, but I hasten to add that their manners were impeccable. They were merely curious."

"In future," said Gruvlax-Xenxa-Schmee, "I would be wary of speaking to strangers..."

"Interesting," Holmes murmured to himself as he settled back in his seat.

At length the air-car came down on the shoulder of another great ziggurat – the Institute of Martian Science itself – and we took an elevator plate down to the ground floor.

"I thought you might care to view the Hall of Technologies Past," said Gruvlax-Xenxa-Schmee, leading us through a high archway to a gloomy chamber the size of an airship hangar. As ever with the interior design of public buildings on Mars, the walls were daubed a uniform taupe and had the pitted appearance of something decorated by insects: again we might have been inside a termite mound. I noticed that we were the only visitors present, and I wondered if Holmes had registered this fact.

More interesting than the lack of decoration, however, were the examples of Martian machinery on display to either side of a central aisle.

First came bulky black, wheeled vehicles, evidently steam-powered, with high cabs and cauldron-like devices set at their front-ends, not unlike the Frenchman, Cugnot's, early steam-driven inventions. As we progressed along the aisle, our host providing a running commentary, it soon became obvious that on Mars, as on Earth, warfare had proved the mother of invention. Again and again we passed ground vehicles and fliers whose purpose was to deliver projectiles, missiles and bombs. Soon we came upon early examples of the kind so horribly familiar to every man, woman and child of Earth: the fearsome tripods. These early versions were smaller, on shorter legs, and with cabins large enough to admit just a single Martian driver.

As we moved from this chamber to the next, we came upon machines that, while they retained the basic shape of the tripod's cowls, yet were without the eponymous three limbs. "And these," Gruvlax-Xenxa-Schmee, "are the latest Martian war machines, which dispense with the rather clumsy tripod locomotion. These are flying machines, which can circumnavigate the globe in a matter of hours."

We made noises to indicate that we were suitably impressed.

Holmes said, "And yet you chose to quell the nations of Earth with the antiquated, three-legged examples of the machine?"

Our guide was quick to correct him. "You refer, of course, to the accursed regime which initiated the unprovoked and unwarranted attack upon your world," it said. "The regime which we have since overthrown..." Gruvlax-Xenxa-Schmee gestured with a tentacle back towards the tripods. "*That* regime," he said, "judged that the tripods would be sufficient to subdue a race which had not yet developed aerial locomotion."

"And were proved correct," Challenger muttered into his beard.

We strolled on, examining what looked like artillery pieces and bulbous rockets. At one point Holmes asked, "How many races dwell upon your planet?"

"Just two, Mr Holmes. We of the equator, the Arkana; and the less populous race of the north, known as the Korchana people."

"And you live in harmony?" Holmes persisted.

"For the most part, though occasional militants from the Korchana people attempt to cause trouble."

"Ah," I said, "the 'terrorists' you mentioned earlier?"

"Just so," said Gruvlax-Xenxa-Schmee, hurrying us along.

We came then to a torpedo-shaped vessel. Unlike every other vehicle we had seen so far, which had been fashioned from pitted materials the hue of graphite, this sleek device was silver.

Gruvlax-Xenxa-Schmee said, "And here we have the prototype of what we call a deep space probe, which we hope to launch on missions to the outer planets of the solar system before too long." He raised an inviting tentacle. "If you would care to step aboard."

Challenger squeezed his considerable girth through the tiny hatch, followed by Holmes. I brought up the rear, glancing back into the grey saucer eyes of our host, who watched me inscrutably.

Within were three fold-down seats facing a console and a blank screen. No sooner had I taken the lead of my friends, and seated myself, than the hatch clanged shut behind me.

I leapt to my feet and searched for some kind of handle on the hatch, to no avail. I pummelled upon the metal surface, calling out, "What is this? Let us out at once, I say!"

Holmes was on his feet, his pistol drawn and his hawk eyes perusing the ceiling for I knew not what.

Challenger bellowed in rage and beat at the metal panels with fists the size of hams.

I fell silent when, seconds later, I heard a peculiar hissing sound, and whirled around to see a mist-like vapour billowing down from the ceiling. My friends, being closer to the source of the gas, had already succumbed and lay sprawled upon the floor. I turned in panic and recommenced my frantic pounding on the hatch.

Then the gas reached me and I, too, slipped into unconsciousness.

I was aware of very little during the next few hours, though I regained my senses for brief, hallucinatory periods.

At one point I was aware of being manhandled, gripped by numerous tentacles and carried along a lighted corridor. Then I was lying on some kind of table, with a blinding light above me, soon occluded by the gargoyle face of a peering Martian. A period of oblivion succeeded this, and next I was aware of being moved at speed, not carried this time, but borne along on something wheeled. I felt tentacles gripping me, lifting me, and then I was deposited on to a shockingly cold surface.

I heard a deafening rumble, as of an engine, and I passed into oblivion and did not resurface for many an hour.

Eight
Imprisoned in the Desert

"Watson! Watson, wake up."

"Wha... what? Where...?"

"Watson," said Holmes. "It's good to have you back in the land of the living."

My friend knelt before me, a hand on my shoulder. I struggled into a sitting position. "Where the blazes are we, Holmes?"

"Where the blazes indeed!" came the bellow from Professor Challenger as he strode back and forth, having discarded his solar topee and his safari jacket. "It's infernally hot in here!"

Holmes assisted me to my feet and I took in our surroundings – or rather, I suspected, our prison.

We were in a great chamber, some hundred yards long by thirty, constructed from the same adobe material as many of the other Martian buildings I had observed. Again the interior was undecorated, and the walls were daubed the usual uniform shade of grey.

There were no openings in the chamber, save one: at the far end of our prison was a semi-circular window as tall as a man at its apex, barred but otherwise open to the elements.

I made my way across to this, accompanied by my friends, and we stared out upon an unprepossessing scene. A red desert stretched away for as far as the eye could see, empty of other buildings and featureless save for the natural rills and ripples created by the ceaseless winds. In the far distance, on the horizon, rose a jagged series of mountains.

The bars were set perhaps nine inches apart, and though I turned myself sideways and attempted to squeeze through the gap, it was to no avail; likewise Holmes, thinner than myself, attempted to force himself between the bars, with the same result. Challenger made no such futile effort: the gap could have been a yard wide, and still not big enough to admit his bulk.

I pulled off my coat and unbuttoned my jacket, then mopped my drenched brow with my kerchief.

"At least out gaolers didn't leave us without fluid," Holmes said, pointing to a nearby stack of cannisters. "Water."

The mere word made me realise how thirsty I was, and I crossed to the six containers, opened one and drank. The water was warm, but served to slake my thirst.

Holmes was pacing the breadth of the chamber before the barred opening, watched closely by Professor Challenger.

"The very fact that the Martians have supplied us with water, but not food," Holmes said at length, "is interesting in itself, and tells me much."

"Such as?" I asked.

"One," said Holmes, "that they do not wish us to die of thirst. They wish to keep us alive, but have placed us here for a very specific reason. Also, we will remain here for a shortish duration only."

"How the deuce do you work that out?" I said.

"If we were to be incarcerated here for any length of time," said he, "then we would have been supplied with food as well as water."

"Very well, but what do they want from us in the shortish time we might be here – and, confound it, where exactly are we?"

Holmes turned to the opening and peered out, frowning, then said, "We are situated on the Amazonis Planitia, perhaps two thousand miles north of the equator, as the mountain you see on the Eastern horizon is none other than Olympus Mons."

"But why in Hell's name have the critters abandoned us here?" Challenger wanted to know.

"I think we will find out," Holmes said, "in due course."

He resumed his pacing, and paused a minute later to ask, "What did you experience immediately after passing out in the silver vehicle back at the Institute of Science? Watson? Challenger?"

I recounted to Holmes the little I could recall; the bright light, the examination of the Martian; being lifted and then ferried on something wheeled; being deposited on a cold surface, and then my final memory: the sound of an engine.

"Evidently belonging to the vehicle that transported us here," said Holmes. "Professor?"

Challenger shrugged his ox-like shoulders. "I was out for the count from the outset," he said. "I do recollect a bright light, but it's as if I dreamed it. I recall nothing else until I awoke in this confounded hole."

"What about you, Holmes?" I asked.

"I recall coming briefly to my senses to find myself on an operating table, as I too was examined by a Martian – they divested me of my pistol, needless to say. I had sufficient wits about me to take in my surroundings, for a few seconds. I received the impression that I was in an operating theatre, and my last recollection is of being inserted, head first, into a vast machine not unlike a blast furnace... After that, nothing."

"But what were the ungodly beasts doing to us, Holmes?" Challenger roared. "By Gad, if I could get my hands on one of the slimy creatures!" And, miming his intent, his huge hairy hands reached out and wrung the next of an imaginary alien.

"I take it that this is your first time on the Red Planet, Professor?" Holmes asked.

"That's right."

"And you were invited here by the diplomat Gruvlax-Xenxa-Schmee?"

Challenger nodded. "Yes."

"For the express purpose of giving a lecture?"

"A couple of talks to the Martian Geographic Society on the subject of my more recent Arabian expeditions."

Holmes stroked his chin. "And did the invitation strike you as... odd, shall I say?"

The big man frowned. "It did cross my mind to wonder how many common or garden Martians might be interested in such a lecture, yes. I might pack the Royal Geographic Society with folk eager to hear my talks, but here on Mars...?" He shrugged.

Holmes said, "I was asked by Gruvlax-Xenxa-Schmee to investigate the murder of a philosopher who, it turns out, does not exist. It appears that we were lured here for reasons other than those we were given. For what purpose, though, remains the question."

"Something to do with... with this 'scanning process' that Hadfield-Bell mentioned?" I ventured.

Holmes nodded. "So it would appear. And it is my supposition that our incarceration, along with our scanning, can only be linked to the larger picture."

"Which is?" Challenger asked.

"The eventual annihilation of the human race," said Holmes.

"But..." I said, "How can that be? The Martians are far in advance of us, technologically. Couldn't they merely wipe us out militarily, if that is their ultimate intent?"

Holmes' brow was buckled in an intense frown of concentration. At last he said, "They could at that. But, perhaps, they do not wish to annihilate us immediately. Invading armies often utilise the subjugated citizens of a defeated nation as labour – slaves, in other words. Perhaps that is the ultimate fate of our kind, and what is happening on Earth now, with the Martians putting on a benign, even altruistic face, is part of a 'softening up' process..."

"And our kidnapping and scanning?" Challenger asked. "Where does that fit into the bigger picture?"

"I must admit, Professor, that on that sore question I am for the moment, though I am loath to admit it, as clueless as yourself."

I moved to the opening and gripped the bars. With all my strength I pulled at them, hoping that the stone in which they were set might crumble – but it was a vain hope. The bars were immovable. And anyway, what purpose might be served by our escape from this chamber? We were in the middle on an inimical desert, after all, a thousand miles from civilisation... And even if we were by some miracle to attain the city of Glench-Arkana, how might we find the means to leave Mars and return to Earth?

My spirit shrivelled at the hopelessness of our situation.

I sat with my back against the wall, sweat trickling down my exhausted face, and withdrew my fob-watch from my waist-coat. Therein I kept a photograph of my dear departed Mary, her sweet smile a boon to my senses in this time of need. I lost myself in a happy reverie of recollection, recalling our time together, our honeymoon in Brighton, and later holidays in the Scottish Highlands. Never had the memory of my country – even when serving in the sere plains of Afghanistan – provoked such a sense of sadness in my heart.

Holmes noticed my mood, and said, "Chin up, Watson. I will refrain from offering such platitudes as 'Where there's life...' But the fact is that all is not yet hopeless. We must be vigilant, and grasp whatever opportunity comes our way."

I was of a mind to say that that was all very well, but the fact remained that we were stranded in a prison in a desert on a planet sixty million miles from home... But I held my tongue and nodded. "You're right, Holmes. There's always hope."

Professor Challenger looked up from where he was seated against the wall opposite me. He cocked his head and said, "Am I going mad, or do I hear the approach of an infernal Martian air-car?"

Holmes bent his ear towards the opening. "I do believe you're right, Professor."

I jumped to my feet and peered through the bars.

Faint at first, and then growing louder, I made out the throb of an engine. I scanned the skies for any sign of the vessel, but saw nothing other than the slow tumble of Phobos far to the north.

Holmes was beside me, and Challenger gripped bars and swore to himself as the engine noise swelled to a deafening volume and the vehicle passed directly overhead.

"There!" cried Holmes, pointing.

A domed air-car came into view and settled on the sands a hundred yards before our gaol. At this distance I could not make out the pilot behind the tinted glass enclosure, and I waited with baited breath for the individual to show itself.

"This is it," Challenger said. "The blighters have come to proposition us – or threaten us. Whatever, I fear that soon we shall learn our fate." He slammed a fist into his meaty palm. "But I for one refuse to go down without a fight!"

"It might not come to fisticuffs," Holmes said. "I advise caution until we learn what the Martians require from us."

"If they ever get round to it," I said, for whoever had piloted the air-car thus far was showing no inclination to climb out and approach our prison.

The air-car sat, a paralysed trilobite, under the ceaseless sun.

An hour elapsed, then two.

"This is intolerable!" Challenger raged. "Are they playing games with us, d'you think?"

"I am at a loss to second guess their motives," Holmes admitted.

Three hours passed since the arrival of the air-car, and the sun, moving overhead and slanting its light now from the west, shone directly into the glass cabin of the vehicle.

I gasped. "Upon my word, Holmes! Look, the vehicle is quite empty."

Holmes and Challenger peered through the bars. "You're right, Watson. There isn't a soul in the driver's seat, nor in the rear."

"But why should our enemies have sent an empty, remote-controlled car?" Challenger mused.

Holmes said, "Perhaps not our enemies, Professor. But our allies?"

"You think someone sent it so that, were we able to escape this chamber...?"

"It seems an odd way to go about achieving our salvation, Watson," he admitted.

Again I fell to struggling with the bars, but I might as well have attempted to uproot an oak tree: they were immovable – and no matter how hard I tried, I could not force myself between the rods of iron. I gave up and slaked my thirst with water.

Ten minutes elapsed. I expected something – I know not what – to happen at any second. But all was still and silent out there, the only sound I heard the occasional imprecation from the professor, and my own thumping heartbeat.

And then, of a sudden, the roar of an engine filled the air, and I rushed back to the opening, fully expecting to see the air-car powering up and taking off.

Instead, a second air-car swooped down from the heavens, approached the opening and hovered before us.

Its pilot leaned forwards, gesturing frantically behind the windscreen for us to move away from the opening.

"By Jove, Holmes!" I cried.

My heart surged with joy, for the pilot, our saviour, was none other than Freya Hadfield-Bell.

Nine
A Simulacrum Revealed

We hurried to the far end of the chamber and turned to watch as Hadfield-Bell reversed the air-car away from the opening.

"How in damnation does the gal hope to get us out of here?" Challenger asked.

"By the only expedient open to her," said Holmes. "Watch."

Hadfield-Bell eased the air-car forward slowly; its front fender came up against the bars. Through the domed windscreen I made out the young woman's face, her features drawn in concentration as she increased power and the air-car pressed forward.

As I watched, three bars bent, and then popped from their moorings with an explosion of shattered stone, and skittered ringing across the stone floor; the air-car surged forward, sending more bars rattling across the chamber, then reversed from the opening and settled in the desert. In a trice Hadfield-Bell leapt from the pilot's seat, climbed on to the dome of the air-car and from there jumped through the opening and into the chamber.

She wore the green uniform of the Martian spaceship line, with the little pill-box hat perched on the side of her head, and I thought I had never seen a more beautiful sight in all my life.

"But how did you find us?" I blurted, rushing forward and taking her hand in gratitude.

"My comrades traced your progress from the Institute and

north to this prison," she said. "We then had to second-guess the motivation of your captors."

"That," said Holmes, "is what has been taxing my thoughts for some time. It occurred to me that we might very well be the bait in a cunning trap."

"In which case," I said in fear, "have the Martians succeeded?"

"You are correct, Mr Holmes," said Hadfield-Bell. "The Martians did indeed sequester you here in an attempt to lure me, or members of the opposition."

"But in that case..." I moaned.

"Fear not, Mr Watson." She smiled at me. "The Martians would not be satisfied with the capture of just a single rebel. They desire far more than that."

"I don't quite follow..."

"When we learned where they had taken you," she said, "we decided to send in an air-car by remote control – to test the waters, as it were. If your Martian captors then pounced, we knew that this was a simple trap designed to capture one or two members of the opposition. If, however, they let it be, then we knew that a much more sophisticated operation was under way."

"And the latter proved to be the case," Holmes said. "But what is that operation?"

Hadfield-Bell paced back and forth, holding her chin. "For a long while the Martian authorities have attempted to locate the rebel's base. They have followed my comrades, recruited spies, employed all manner of devious means to root out and destroy those Martians which oppose their draconian rule – but to no avail. We have always remained one step ahead of them. However... I suspect that we were observed, or overheard, by government spies in the restaurant in Glench-Arkana, and they devised a scheme to sequester you here... as bait."

Her lips formed a stern line as she looked from one to the other of us. "We had a comrade in the Institute," she said, "who reported that you three had been scanned, and that you were unconscious for an hour or two afterwards. That was all the time they required to put their plan into action."

"Their plan?" I echoed.

Hadfield-Bell pulled a device from the pocket of her jacket. It was a small, square object, about the size of a cigarette case, but jet black. Set into its upper fascia was a tiny screen, which she peered down at intently.

What happened next not only surprised but shocked me. Professor Challenger, one moment at my side, at the next leaped forward with a deafening bellow and dashed the device from the woman's grip. "No!"

The device flew through the air and skittered across the stone floor, and Challenger, like a man possessed, dived after it. I watched in shock, hardly able to believe my eyes, as Hadfield-Bell in lightning reaction leapt towards the professor and, with a display of acrobatics I later learned was termed ju-jitsu, swivelled in the air and lashed out with her right leg. Her shod foot caught Challenger in the midriff and with a mighty gust of expelled air he barrelled backwards and hit the wall. She lost no time in diving for the device, snatching it up, and backing away from Challenger as he staggered forward and gathered himself to attack.

"What's possessed you, man!" I cried. "She rescued us, for pity's sake! Can't you see that she's on our side?"

As Challenger surged towards her, Hadfield-Bell drew a second device from her pocket and directed it at the professor. This was a handgun, and had the immediate effect of bringing Challenger up short.

His consternation was short-lived, however. In the act of raising his arms into the air, he dived sideways towards me, gripped me about the neck and then so manhandled me as to put my body between himself and Hadfield-Bell. I was now, in effect, a shield.

Moreover, he fastened his meaty fingers around my neck and called out, "One move and Watson is dead!"

"Have you taken leave of your senses, man!" I choked.

"Unhand me at once!"

His fingers increased their grip on my throat.

Holmes took one step towards me, rage and knowledge of his impotence twisting his features.

"I never had you down as a traitor to the human race, Challenger," said he. "You, of all men, I would have thought loyal to king and country. What possessed you, Professor? What twisted motive made you to throw your lot in with the Martians?"

Hadfield-Bell stepped forward. She, of all of us, seemed in charge of the situation: her demeanour possessed an enviable *sang froid* as she smiled across at Challenger. "Would you care to answer Mr Holmes' question, or shall I tell them?"

"We shall prevail!" Challenger bellowed. "We invaded Earth for good reason, and we shall prove ultimately victorious! The perfidy of the opposition, in attempting to waylay our master-plan, is misguided and short-lived!"

"You say 'we'?" Holmes said. "How can you align yourself with our oppressors, Professor? Consider how the people of England might view you, a hero of the nation, a man decorated and feted for his unswerving devotion to the Empire... grovelling now at the feet of tyrants! What have they promised you, Challenger? Wealth, power – the means to explore the solar system at your leisure?"

Challenger growled, his fingers tightening on my oesophagus.

I fought for breath, but my lungs were bursting and my vision failing...

Hadfield-Bell seemed preoccupied, attending to whatever was displayed upon the screen of the device. She smiled to herself, then looked up at me. She lifted the weapon in her right hand and aimed it in my direction.

"Dr Watson," she said calmly, "I apologise in advance..."

And so saying, she lifted the handgun a fraction and fired.

I expected to hear the deafening report of a bullet, but heard instead the sharp crackle of an electrical current. And instead of a bullet, there issued from the handgun a bright blue light which missed me by a fraction and hit Professor Challenger square on the forehead. He cried out, electrocuted, and in that instant I too felt the pain of the charge conducted through his hands, though diminished. Challenger released his grip on my throat and fell to the floor, choking. I staggered, reeling, across the chamber. Holmes caught me and lowered me into a sitting position against the wall, and together we watched as the next act of the drama was played out.

Hadfield-Bell strode across the chamber and stood over the prostrate form of Professor Challenger, staring down at him with neither pity nor revulsion on her face. Business-like, she replaced the screen-device in the pocket of her jacket, slipped the handgun under her belt, and drew a knife.

She knelt before the professor and, as I watched in horror, thrust the blade into the professor's throat. With a savage downward motion, she opened the man's torso from pharynx to abdomen.

I expected blood, of course, and was wholly unprepared for what did emerge from the gaping wound – which was precisely nothing.

Holmes left my side and joined Hadfield-Bell, kneeling to closer examine her handiwork.

I struggled to my feet and, still reeling from the after-effects of the electrocution, joined them.

Hadfield-Bell had taken a firm grip on the flesh to either side of the gaping wound and, as I watched, ripped open the chest cavity.

I stared, disbelieving, as I attempted to work out quite what I was looking at.

Not blood and bone, or glistening musculature or adipose tissue, no – but masses of wires and circuitry and silver anodes.

"What the...?" I began.

Hadfield-Bell smiled up at me. "Not Professor Challenger," she said, "but a devious simulacrum."

Holmes said, under his breath, "I begin to see..."

Hadfield-Bell climbed to her feet, dusting her palms together and staring down at what I still thought of as Professor Challenger. "The Martians, in 'scanning' you three at the Institute, were creating what they call 'cognitive copies' – in other words, copies of your minds, your personalities, which they then downloaded into mechanical simulacra."

"You mean," I gasped, "they made copies of me and Holmes, too? But...?"

She smiled. "Don't worry – in case you're wondering, you are the originals."

"My word, that's good to know, Holmes, isn't it?"

He smiled to himself, then addressed Hadfield-Bell, "And they switched the real Professor for this copy in order to carry out their scheme to entrap you and your comrades?"

"Precisely," she replied. She nodded at the simulacrum. "I suspect that somewhere amid all that machinery is a beacon, relaying to the Martians its precise whereabouts."

"But what now?" I asked.

She gave a winning grin. "Our spy at the Institute informed us that Professor Challenger was taken, still unconscious, from the building and imprisoned in the city gaol. When we worked out just what trick the Martians were playing, we devised a counter-plan of our own – which was another reason we sent in the first air-car. Now, if you would be so good as to help me drag the simulacrum to that vehicle."

We bent and took hold of the unholy creature, and I must admit that the sensation of gripping its clammy ersatz flesh – some kind of life-like rubber compound – was altogether sickening.

Holmes and I took a foot each and, with Hadfield-Bell gripping its arms, we hauled the body towards the arched opening and with little ceremony pushed it through and on to the sand a yard beneath. We then jumped down and dragged the thing across to the first air-car. Hadfield-Bell opened the pilot's door and we heaved the bulk of the fake Challenger into the front seat.

Panting at the exertion, she mopped sweat from her brow and stared about the cloudless sky. "And now," she said, "to send our enemy on a wild goose chase, as it were..."

She ducked into the cockpit of the air-car, ran an expert hand across the control console, then stepped back smartly and slammed the door shut. We retreated as the engine powered up and the vehicle rose into the air, banked and accelerated in a westerly direction. Soon it was but a dwindling dot in the alien sky.

"That should keep them busy for a day or two, until the fuel runs out and it crash-lands – and oh, wouldn't I like to see the expressions on their faces when they find the wreckage of the air-car and realise that their devious scheme has come to nothing!"

I stared at her. "You can detect expressions on their hideous faces?" I laughed.

"I was speaking metaphorically, Doctor." She gestured across to the second air-car. "After you, gentlemen."

We had scarcely settled ourselves in the back seat of the vehicle, and Hadfield-Bell taken the controls and lifted us into the air, when Holmes leaned forward and said, "So the Martians have made copies – simulacra – of Watson and myself..." He mused a while, then went on, "But what I would like to know, Miss Hadfield-Bell, is why?"

She looked over her shoulder, tossing her blonde tresses, and graced us with a beautiful smile. "I will explain that, Mr Holmes, and much more besides, when we come to journey's end. You have had a trying few hours, and must be exhausted. I advise you to try and sleep for the remainder of the flight."

I thought that a capital idea, and sank back into the padded seat as Hadfield-Bell flew us at speed towards the northern fastness of the Martian rebels.

Ten
Miss Hadfield-Bell Explains

I woke with a start some time later, and heard Hadfield-Bell call from the pilot's seat, "My apologies. We hit a little turbulence back there."

"That's quite all right," Holmes replied. "I was awake already, though I think the good doctor's slumber was disturbed."

"I feel well rested," I said, stretching in my seat. "I say, how long have we been aloft?"

"A little over six hours," Hadfield-Bell replied. "We should arrive at Zenda-Zenchan in less than an hour."

Holmes repeated the name. "The capital city of the rebels?"

"That's right – one of the few remaining, thanks to the relentless bombing carried out by the Arkana."

I peered through the side window to my left; far below, the red sands stretched to the curved horizon, the only interruption being a low range of mountains to the west and, straight ahead, a lake similar to the body of water I had witnessed from the *Valorkian* on our arrival on Mars. However, as we approached the 'lake' and overflew it, I saw that my vision had been tricked. The shimmering silver expanse was not a lake at all, but a vast flat plain of glass like the roof of a gigantic hothouse. Here and there across its scintillating surface I made out dark jagged gashes or rents, where the glass had been smashed.

"What the blazes is that?" I asked, pointing.

Hadfield-Bell peered down. "That is the abandoned city of Kalthera-Jarron," she said. "It was once the second largest city of the Korchana people, until the Arkana bombed it to oblivion. You see the damage where the atom-missiles struck. The chaos caused far below, in the city itself, and the loss of life occasioned twenty years ago, was truly horrific."

"But why were the Arkana and the Korchana at war?" Holmes asked.

Hadfield-Bell smiled, sadly. "For the same reason that wars occur on Earth," she said. "The two peoples are ideologically opposed. This was not a war over territory, though that did come into it, so much as two implacably opposing views on how to manage the future of the Martian people."

"Intriguing," Holmes murmured. "And what were these mutually exclusive ideologies?"

"For you to fully understand that," she said, "first I must explain something about the cosmological situation of the Red Planet. You see, for as long as the Martian race has been technologically 'civilised', that is, for the past five hundred years, scientists have been aware that Mars is moving slowly but inexorably away from the sun; this has the double effect of making the surface of the planet ever cooler, and reducing the oxygen content of the atmosphere. For a few hundred years, the ability of Martian scientists to do anything to effect a change in the situation was scant; however, with the advance of their science, methods have been devised whereby the future of the planet and its people was made secure. Engineers from the northern university at Zenda-Zenchan came up with a means of making many of their cities hermetic by covering them with glass roofs – such as you saw back there. Also, scientists devised machines which could extract oxygen from the very rock itself, and in so doing employ the planet as 'lungs', as it were. This was a cripplingly expensive scheme, but one which would ensure the survival of the race. The northern cities underwent a transformation; it helped that many of them were already ensconced in great rift valleys or fissures. The cities of the equator were built upon flat plains, however, and moving them and their populations to vast, pre-built underground domiciles proved more problematic, as well as costly. So the politicians of the equator came up with an alternative solution."

Holmes nodded sagely. "Allow me to hazard a guess – not something I am usually wont to do," said he. "The equatorial politicians suggested that a wholesale removal of their people to the neighbouring world, namely Earth, might prove a more practical solution to their problems?"

"Exactly so," said Hadfield-Bell. "They saw that planet Earth was an ideal refuge. It possessed just the right mix of oxygen and nitrogen in its atmospheric make-up, had bountiful supplies of raw materials, vast uninhabited tracts of land, and a population that was relatively technologically unsophisticated. So the peaceful solution of the northerners was ignored, and preparations were made for the invasion of Earth.

"At the same time as the first armadas set sail for Earth, the Arkana declared war on the states of the north, in a blood-lust fuelled, no doubt, by the prospect of their imminent victory over we humans. But their triumph was premature."

"And all on our planet duly rejoiced!" said I.

"In the months that followed," Hadfield-Bell went on, "the Arkana set about creating antibodies to combat terrestrial diseases, and in due course they set off again for Earth. Since the first invasion, however, the Martians had taken the time to reconsider the *modus operandi* of their invasion. Rather than expend money and valuable resources on conquering Earth militarily, it was decided that they would cow our planet by ostensibly peaceful means, and so came masquerading as altruistic benefactors – a ruse that pulled the wool over the eyes of the leaders of our planet."

She paused to point through the glass. "There, on the horizon, is what remains of the city of Zenda-Zenchan. We will make landfall nearby and head for a system of tunnels where my rebel comrades have their base."

The air-car banked, and I held on as we swooped through the air towards the surface of the desert.

"And the ultimate aim of the equatorial Martians," Holmes said, "is to take control of our world until such time as all opposition has been wiped out and they can effect the mass transfer of their citizens to Earth?"

"That is the situation in a nutshell, Mr Holmes," said Hadfield-Bell. "Already they are moving their attention away from the war against the Korchana, and concentrating on Earth. Now we will land, take sustenance, and plan the next phase of our journey."

"The next phase..." I echoed. "To where, exactly?"

"Back to Glench-Arkana," she said. "But more of that later."

She frowned in concentration as she brought the air-car in low over sand-sculpted dunes, decelerated, and landed on a featureless swathe of sand as fine and red as paprika. As we climbed from the vehicle, emerging into the merciless heat of the evening sun, I saw a dark patch in the side of a nearby dune, and no sooner had I set eyes upon this feature than a dozen or more small, dark-skinned Martians emerged from the tunnel and scuttled across to the air-car. Amid much waving of tentacles, and high-pitched Martian greetings, we were surrounded by the Korchana people, and Hadfield-Bell bent to embrace certain individuals and speak to them in their staccato tongue.

She laughed and turned to us. "They are overjoyed to see us," she explained, "as they feared that we'd been captured and killed. This way."

Buoyed along by the crowd, we followed the woman across the sand and into the welcome shade of the tunnel. When my vision adjusted, assisted by strip-lighting that illuminated the tunnel at intervals of twenty feet, I saw that we were hurrying down a steeply sloping mineshaft shored up by metal girders. Soon the sandy surface underfoot gave way to ringing metal, and as if by some miracle – for surely we had descended a hundred yards beneath the surface of the planet already? – daylight shone ahead of us. We came out on to a great gallery running along the edge of a vast chasm, and I looked up to see an extensive honeycomb awning of glass, through which the setting sun cast its rufous rays. We were in the bomb-blasted city of Zenda-Zenchan.

I glanced to my left, over the gallery rail, and wished that I had not given in to my curiosity. The chasm seemed bottomless, and my head swam vertiginously. Far below, I made out the fire-blackened ruins of gallery after gallery.

Hadfield-Bell turned right, down a wide, burnt-out corridor. She came to a double door and pushed it open, standing aside so that we could enter. The room was large and sun-lit – its far wall comprised a single floor-to-ceiling window that overlooked the chasm and was illuminated by sunlight slanting in through the glass roof high above.

"You will find hot running water," she said, pointing to an arrangement of brass piping and a large water tank. "I suggest that you refresh yourself and meet me, next door, in thirty minutes. We have much to discuss."

With this, she withdrew from the room, taking with her three or four curious Martians.

I stripped to the waist, ran a tank full of hot water, and proceeded to wash myself with a great scouring sponge no doubt designed for Martian skin, and handfuls of liquid soap. Holmes, for his part, merely paced back and forth, lost in introspection.

I dried myself on a towel five times the size of a bath-towel, donned my old and somewhat sweat-stained clothing, and joined Holmes at the window.

He was gazing down at the wreckage with a lugubrious expression.

"A race which can visit such death and destruction to its own kind," he said, "will have no qualms about wiping out the entirety of mankind. The 'second wave' have treated us with kid gloves so far, Watson, but judging by what Hadfield-Bell has told us, that will not continue. As soon as they have gathered sufficient materiel and turned their attention from subjugating their own..." He did not finish.

A communicating door opened, and a Martian appeared. He fluted something, to which Holmes replied in kind. "Hadfield-Bell is ready," he said, "and a 'council of war' has convened. We had better join them."

We followed the Martian through the door into a large room dominated by a low, oval brass table; around it, on cushions, were seated a dozen dark-skinned Martians, and as we crossed the room and took vacant cushions to the left and right of Hadfield-Bell, twenty-four great grey eyes charted our progress in silence.

Immediately we were seated, half a dozen voices spoke up, seemingly speaking across each other in high passion: it was a wonder that any sense could be made of the din, but Hadfield-Bell pitched into the debate, held forth for long minutes, and a silence descended as she spoke and all those around the table listened to what she had to say.

At last she gestured, and others spoke, and she turned to us and murmured, "They were debating how we should proceed – they had two or three different proposals. I suggested a way forward, and they are debating this now. I think it only a matter of time before a consensus is agreed upon."

Holmes said, "Which brings me back to my earlier question, Miss Hadfield-Bell – what are the Martian's motives in making copies of Challenger, Watson, and myself?"

"It is all part of their master-plan, Mr Holmes. To smooth the way for their ultimate invasion, they need the assistance of the human race itself – and how better to achieve that than to 'copy' certain individuals of influence?"

"You mean –?"

Hadfield-Bell gave an assenting frown. "Over the course of the past few years," she said, "how many world leaders have accepted invitations to visit the Red Planet?"

At her words, a great weight settled in my stomach, and an even greater weight upon my soul.

"I would say," said Holmes grimly, "that almost every leader of note has at some point made the journey."

"And not returned," she said, glancing from Holmes to myself. "Oh, to all intents and purposes they come back to Earth with great tales of the scientific wonders they have beheld, and highfalutin notions of peace between our peoples, but..."

"But these are copies," Holmes said grimly, "simulacra of our leaders, planted to do the bidding of their masters when the time finally comes for the final push of Martian forces."

My senses swam at the very idea, and at length I brought myself to ask the question, "But... but what became of the originals? Why, just last year Campbell-Bannerman made the journey."

Hadfield-Bell gazed down at her hands on the table-top, and murmured, "What do you think became of our Prime Minister, and all the others, Doctor? They were interrogated, milked of every last shred of information they possessed, and then... dispatched."

I closed my eyes briefly, sickened. Holmes, not a man much given to profanity, swore quietly to himself.

Hadfield-Bell went on, "They copy and send forth not only world leaders and influential business-men and scientists, but leaders in other fields, too, whom they think might be able to assist the goal of world domination. Thus the world-famous zoologist and explorer Professor Challenger was abducted, along with the world's finest detective, and his accomplice, Sherlock Holmes and Doctor Watson, as well as artists, actors and many other unfortunate souls."

"So poor Challenger...?" Holmes began.

"I have intelligence from our agents that the Professor met his end shortly after he was taken to the Glench-Arkana gaol," she said. "Apparently he attacked a Martian when they interrogated him, and he was summarily despatched."

I hung my head at the thought of the death of such a brave man. "May his death not have been in vain," I murmured.

Holmes leaned forward. "You mentioned that we would return to Glench-Arkana," said he.

Hadfield-Bell held up a hand and said, "One moment, please."

She spoke in Martian, and silenced the twitters around the table. She fired off what sounded like questions to various individuals, and nodded at their replies.

Minutes later she turned to us and said, "A way forward has been agreed. As we speak, the Arkana are preparing to send the simulacra of yourselves back to Earth on the next ship, scheduled to leave Mars in just over a day from now. Once arrived on Earth, your doubles will resume your old life in 221B Baker Street, as if nothing untoward has occurred – conveying information to their masters and awaiting the call to assist the ultimate invasion. Meanwhile, the Arkana will stop at nothing in their search for you, the originals." She looked from Holmes to myself, with steel in her bright blue eyes. "We must at all costs ensure that they do not succeed in transporting your simulacra to Earth. To this end, we will apprehend them and make the switch – insinuating yourselves in their place – without their guards suspecting a thing. We will then despatch the simulacra, and you can proceed to Earth as double agents, so to speak."

"A tall order," Holmes opined.

"A tall order indeed, sir. The only alternative – and we might be forced into it, if all does not go well – would be to send you two back to Earth aboard a vessel we have readied here. But I will be honest and tell you that the vessel is old and not a little unsafe, and our technicians not of the finest..." She paused, and then went on, "And then, once you have returned to Earth, you must overcome your doubles and take their place... Either that, or go into hiding and take on disguises so that the Martian authorities do not learn of your return."

Holmes said, "If we fail to make the switch with our

doppelgängers in Glench-Arkana, then to leave for Earth aboard the substandard ship is a risk that we must take. We *must* return to Earth, to continue the fight against our Martian oppressors."

"Hear, hear!" I called out.

Hadfield-Bell gave a thin-lipped smile. "Excellent. We will proceed to Glench-Arkana forthwith and effect the switch. To that end..." She called out in Martianese, and a pair of aliens who had been guarding the entrance hurried out and returned, a minute later, hauling what at first I assumed were three captive Martians.

They dropped the captives before the table, and I saw that they were not captives at all, but rubber suits.

"I am afraid," said Hadfield-Bell, "that if we are to succeed in the next step of the operation, we must travel to Glench-Arkana in disguise."

I stared down at the macabre sight of the flopping rubber Martians prostrated at my feet, and I could not help but laugh.

Eleven
Disaster Strikes

Hadfield-Bell, an expert in the utilisation of the suits, helped us into our rubber disguises. They opened via long lateral slits at the back of the head-torsos: while she held the suit steady, I wriggled feet-first through the gap and worked my legs into the two thicker, central tentacles. I could not stand upright, of course, due to the short stature of the average Martian, but was forced to assume an uncomfortable crouching position, working my head into a gap in the front of the suit and ensuring that I could see through a flap of gauze material positioned just behind the beak or mouth of the creature. A series of levers to my left and right working the supernumerary forward and aft tentacles, as well as opening and closing the beak. Locomotion was achieved by moving one's lower legs in an excruciating series of shuffles. Hadfield-Bell nodded judiciously and declared that we would pass muster, then donned her own suit.

"The situation is this," she said an hour later as she piloted us south. "The Martians are holding your simulacra in a safe-house close to the spaceport. We have spies in place, monitoring the situation. The next ship scheduled to leave for Earth will lift-off at fourteen o'clock, in just four hours from now. The simulacra will be transferred to the ship just one hour before it departs. The Martian authorities have no reason to suspect any trouble, and

the simulacra will be attended by the normal level of security –
that is, no more than two armed guards."

I stared through the glass at the land passing far below; a
ruler-straight canal arrowed towards the horizon, dotted with all
manner of sailing craft.

"Our task of defeating the invaders," Holmes observed, "is
made all the more difficult due to the fact that among our own
kind are the simulacra, scheming to further the ends of the
Martians."

"The good news on that front," Hadfield-Bell replied, "is
that, thanks to the network of spies in Glench-Arkana, we know
who these mechanical imposters are. The difficulty will be to
neutralise them without alerting our Martian overlords, and
persuading other high-ups in the military and government of the
fact of the duplicity."

"On the face of it," I said, "that appears a hopeless task."

"All is not hopeless, Dr Watson," said Hadfield-Bell. "The
forces of the north, though punished heavily in the war, are not
defeated: they have armaments and citizens aplenty with which to
oppose the Arkana. Also, among the ranks of the equatorial
Martians there are those who oppose the barbarity of their
fellows. Together we can overcome our oppressors and rid the
planet of the Martian menace."

"Well said," Holmes applauded. "And we can do our bit by
succeeding in vanquishing our own simulacra and taking their
places. I for one relish the task ahead."

I stared through the glass and wished that I could be as
sanguine as my friend.

In due course the ugly spires and domes of Glench-Arkana hove
into sight, sectioned by the spoke-like roads and streets which
converged on the central spaceport. Hadfield-Bell brought the
air-car down beside a quiet canal before a terrace of low
dwellings constructed of the ubiquitous dark-grey material. The

only splash of colour was provided by flowering vines which climbed the frontage of the buildings.

To our right, beyond the canal, was the corrugated grey perimeter wall of the spaceport. Beyond, the towering nose-cones of Martian spaceships loomed, standing tall beside ugly web-work gantries. Terminal buildings, bending like scimitars embedded blade-first into the ground, gave the skyline a wholly exotic appearance.

Hadfield-Bell consulted her watch, then pointed a tentacle at a section of terrace thirty yards along the street. "That building, sporting the rather loud red tulip-like blooms, is the safe-house."

"Just what is the plan?" Holmes asked, his voice muffled.

"The simulacra are in the safe-house," she said, "watched over by two security guards. However, in a little over ten minutes, two guards from the spaceport will collect your copies for the short journey to the ship that will take them to Earth. These second guards are Korchana sympathisers. They will take custody of the simulacra in their air-car, and we will follow them to a quiet area of the city. There they will deactivate the simulacra, and you will take their place. You will proceed with the guards to the ship, and in a week will once again be on Earth. But do not worry," she added, "we will have spies aboard the ship who will administer you with the sedative for the journey."

"And you?" I asked.

"I will remain here, working for the rebel cause in whatever capacity I can."

As we waited, my thoughts strayed to Professor Challenger and all the other innocent humans who had been lured to their deaths on the Red Planet. I thought of Campbell-Bannerman, our Prime Minister, and Roosevelt from the States, and the leaders of many European nations. I recalled that just last year the press had made much of Field Marshall Kitchener's voyage to Mars – being the first military man granted the privilege – and before that writers such as Jules Verne and H. G. Wells had accepted invitations to lecture there... I thought of Shaw and

Chesterton, whom I had listened to at Hyde Park little more than a week ago: I wondered if they had been informed, by the rebels, of the imposition of the simulacra?

It struck me, as I sat in the back of the air-car, my pulse racing, that the situation was bleak: great forces were ranged against us, and our resistance seemed puny by comparison. At least – I cheered myself with the thought – we had feisty individuals like Freya Hadfield-Bell with whom to share the fight.

"Two minutes to go," she reported.

In due course an air-car landed in the street outside the safe-house, and two Martians climbed from the vehicle and approached the house. One of them pressed a panel beside the door with its tentacle, then stood back and waited.

The door opened; the hideous face of a Martian appeared, ogling the pair with its huge grey eyes. Conversation passed between the aliens, and I awaited the appearance of the simulacra. Truth to tell, I was more than a little curious at the notion of looking upon a copy of myself...

"What's taking so long...?" Hadfield-Bell said at one point. "The hand-over was arranged at the highest level – the authorities should have no cause for suspicion."

The two rebel guards passed what looked to be official papers over to the house guard, who scrutinised the documents. A second house guard appeared, and the first passed the papers to it.

"Make haste..." Hadfield-Bell exhorted.

At last, the house-guards stepped aside, apparently satisfied, and gestured back into the building. At this, two familiar figures stepped through the doorway and joined the rebel guards.

The sight of myself and Holmes left me speechless. Holmes was as I had always seen him, an exact replica down to his precise gait and the way he held his head – but their version of myself? Was I really that short, and portly; and did I comport myself with such a rush, and on such short legs?

I did my best to banish vanity and watch as the bodyguards

led the imposters across the street towards their air-car.

Just as I was thinking that the operation was going without a hitch, one of the house-guards called out something which made the rebel pair stop in their tracks and turn. The house-guards stepped into the street and faced the rebels. A lengthy altercation ensued.

"What's happening?" I asked.

"I don't like this one bit..." was all Hadfield-Bell would say.

As we watched, my heartbeat rapid, one of the house-guards pulled a weapon from a bandolier around its torso and waved it at the rebels.

"I can only assume that they found some irregularity with the false documentation," she muttered. "I must do something..."

And, so saying, she reached out a tentacle, opened the door and before we could say a word to make her think again, slipped from the vehicle and hurried along the street.

I leaned forward, sweating all the more in the infernal Martian suit. "What the bally hell is the girl doing!" I cried.

Beside me, Holmes urged caution. "I am sure she has plan of action."

Hadfield-Bell approached the four aliens and two simulacra, evidently speaking to the house-guards in their native tongue. It was obvious that this was a pre-arranged tactic of diversion – for as the house-guards turned to address the newcomer, the rebel pair acted. One drew a weapon and shot the first house-guards dead, then turned it upon the second.

"But what's this!" Holmes cried, pointing a tentacle.

I stared in horror as at least four Martians tumbled from the safe-house, drawing weapons and attacking the rebels – and attacking, also, Freya Hadfield-Bell. She threw herself to the floor and rolled towards her attacker, skittling it in short order and regaining her feet.

While this was going on, another air-car arrived upon the scene, a larger one this time which disgorged half a dozen Martians – Korchana or Arkana, I was unable to discern – who flung themselves into the melee.

The fighting was hand to hand now, with tentacles flailing and only occasionally a Martian able to use its weapon with any certitude.

Soon I found it impossible to tell friend from foe as squat aliens fought in the street. An incongruous sight amid the carnage, however, was the simulacra: either deactivated by the house-guards, or finding themselves in a situation they had not been programmed to handle, they stood stock still like shop-window mannequins while the battle raged about them.

At one point in the fight, Hadfield-Bell fell to the ground and lay still. At first I thought that she had fallen victim to the assault, but Holmes cried out, "No! Look..."

The suit that contained the woman was moving, and I knew then what she was doing. Useless in combat within the suit, she was attempting to squirm from it.

I was almost beside myself with apprehension. I would rather she played dead, and survived, than take it upon herself to play the hero!

Duly Hadfield-Bell succeeded in fighting free of the suit, and emerged – like a beautiful butterfly from an ugly chrysalis – into the fray.

"No..." I wept as she pulled a weapon and fired at an advancing alien.

She missed, and her attacker raised its weapon. Hadfield-Bell, displaying her skill at ju-jitsu she had first exhibited in the desert, pirouetted and lashed out a long leg, catching the alien its face and sending it sprawling across the street. She ducked the blow of an advancing alien, raised her weapon and shot it dead.

Unable to help himself, Holmes tried to open the door, crying, "No!"

Despite sharing Holmes' fears for the safety of the girl, I knew the folly of embroiling ourselves in the melee, and I reached out a tentacle and restrained my friend. "We can do nothing, Holmes, other than needlessly sacrifice ourselves!"

We watched in mounting horror as yet another air-car descended. Six burly brutes jumped out and joined the fray, and for the next thirty seconds all was the whirl of confusion as shots rang out and perhaps two dozen aliens lashed at each other with flying tentacles.

"Freya!" I cried out, more to myself, "run!"

She looked around her in desperation as the Martians converged, and I was willing her to take to her heels when a Martian drew a weapon and, with a deliberation terrible to behold, fired at her from close range. She staggered backwards, clutching at the ragged hole in the centre of her chest – her eyes wide with terrible shock – and tumbled backwards on to the ground.

I cried out and, despite my earlier reservations, scrambled out into the street.

Before I could reach the dying woman, however, I felt strong tentacles impede my progress. I struggled, assuming that Holmes was the agent of my arrest – but saw that he was struggling with his own captors. I fell to the ground, the impact softened by the thick padding, and looked along the level of the street to where Freya Hadfield-Bell lay inert, her glassy eyes staring lifelessly into space.

Stricken, I gave in to my captors and allowed myself to be dragged along the street, whereupon I was unceremoniously bundled into the back of an air-car the size of a pantechnicon. Holmes landed landed beside me with a grunt and the doors were slammed shut and locked. Seconds later the roar of engines and a certain buoyancy told us that we were airborne.

I thought of Professor Challenger, and all the other humans who had fallen foul of the merciless Martians, and though I knew that it was my fate to join them, I felt little personal fear, numbed as I was by what I had seen occur in the street mere seconds ago.

A part of me disbelieving still, I said, "I should never have stopped you, Holmes! Had we acted upon your impulses we might have saved her life..."

Holmes was struggling from his Martian suit. His head and torso emerged, and he said, "You did right in restraining me, Watson. Don't berate yourself on that score. We could have done nothing. Did you see how many of them there were down there? It would have been folly to have joined in the fray."

"Any more futile than the position we now find ourselves in?" I asked. "At least we would have gone down with a fight!"

"The end result would have been the same, my friend."

I pulled off my suit and cast it aside in disgust, choking with emotion. "I'll tell you this much, Holmes. I will avenge her death! So help me God, I will! I will go down fighting, whenever the monsters show themselves!"

A sound issued from the far end of the small chamber, and Holmes said, "It would seem that you do not have long to wait."

I looked up as a tentacled beast shambled into the rear of the pantechnicon, then stopped a couple of yards away and regarded us with its great glaucous eyes.

I rose to my feet, ready to leap at the first opportunity.

The monster's beak moved, and it addressed us in its meaningless, high-pitched jabber.

Meaningless to me, at least – but not to Holmes.

I was on the point of throwing myself at the creature when my friend flung back his head and laughed.

I stared at Holmes in mystification. "Have you taken leave...?"

He pointed at the Martian. "The Martian is a Korchana, Watson. A rebel. It apologises for the failure of the operation, and says that it is taking us to the city of Zenda-Zenchan, where its compatriots are readying a ship to take us back to Earth."

Thereupon, the terrible events of the day finally catching up with me, I fell to my knees and wept.

There was little to report of the next few hours; I passed them in a state of numbed disbelief, too grief-stricken to appreciate the miracle of my salvation, and perhaps even then feeling a nascent guilt at having survived the ordeal while Freya Hadfield-Bell had not.

We made it to the northern city of Zenda-Zenchan as the setting sun lay down a patina of marmalade hues, and were thence ferried by land-car through the tunnels and galleries of the subterranean city until we emerged into an open-air bowl in the centre of which stood, proud yet battered, a small ship.

We were escorted to our berths and submerged in the gel that would cosset us for the week-long duration of our flight to Earth, and the Martian rebel looked from me to Holmes and addressed my friend.

"What was that, Holmes?" I asked listlessly as I drank down the sedative offered by a second alien.

"He says that we will land somewhere in northern France, where the presence of the occupying Martians is scant. By that time, our simulacra will be ensconced in Baker Street. He will supply us with electrical guns so that we can despatch the simulacra when we reach London, and in due course an agent of the Martian rebels will be in touch to plan the way ahead."

I nodded. "Very well."

I watched as the Martian raised a tentacle in farewell, then backed from the tiny room.

I recalled Freya Hadfield-Bell's words about the safety of this vessel, and said, "Of course, Holmes, we might never make it home, you know..."

And a part of me, as I spoke these words, welcomed the thought of sliding into the balm of oblivion, never to emerge.

I was still gripped by grief when the engine thundered deafeningly and the sedative finally took effect.

Twelve
Confrontation at 221B Baker Street

It was strange indeed to be back upon the planet of my birth, where the air was fresh and the gravity tugged greedily at my body. It took us a good few hours, as we left the ship in a forest outside Dieppe and made our way towards the harbour, to gain our land legs and take in the fact of our having survived the perilous sixty million mile voyage from the Red Planet.

We took a steam packet from Dieppe, and I considered what lay ahead, the hopeless struggle against our oppressors; perhaps my thoughts were still burdened by the fate of Freya Hadfield-Bell, for I had to admit that I had little heart for the fight. It all seemed so hopeless, even futile, without the shining light of her indomitable spirit to guide the way.

Six hours after touching down in France we pulled into Waterloo station, from whence we made haste to the town-house of Sherlock's brother, Mycroft.

We lodged with him that evening, and over a substantial dinner Holmes recounted our adventures on the Red Planet, then went on to outline our imminent assault on the accursed simulacra.

On this latter point, however, Mycroft was unsure: he counselled us to caution, and suggested we go into hiding and think through our options.

Over a lavish breakfast the following morning, before we were due to set off to Baker Street, he again begged us to consider our actions. "You would be much safer assuming other identities and living incognito," he said. "Quite apart from the dangers inherent in broaching this pair, you will be forced into assuming your old roles – and how long might it be before the Martians learnt that you are not indeed their simulacra? Then the fat will be in the fire."

Holmes considered his brother's words, then replied, "The alternative, living incognito as you say, will mean that to all intents and purposes the world famous pairing of Holmes and Watson will be free to do the evil bidding of our overlords – and who knows what nefarious activities they might embark upon! At least, with the simulacra out of the way, we will prevent that. And if things take a turn for the worse and the Martians become wise to our ruse, then we will do as you counsel, go to earth and assume other identities."

"So there is no way I might talk you out of this course of action, Sherlock?"

"No way at all," said my friend.

"In that case, allow me to assist you in bagging this pair," said Mycroft.

Two hours later, Holmes and I, disguised as chimney sweeps with all the requisite paraphernalia in tow, and blackened faces into the bargain, sat drinking strong tea in a workman's café around the corner from Baker Street. Mycroft was stationed in an electrical cab a little way along the street from 221B, from where he had seen the simulacra depart the house at ten that morning. A street urchin, with half a crown for his pains, was at the ready to convey Mycroft's word to us just as soon as the pair returned.

It was now noon, and no word from the runner...

I was in a state of nervous apprehension.

"All will be well, Watson. It will be, as the saying goes, a turkey shoot. The simulacra are expecting no assault, and likely will be unarmed. And..." He patted his jacket pocket where he carried his electrical gun, "with these weapons we cannot fail."

I nodded, reassured by his words and the weight of the weapon in my own pocket.

Minutes later the café door opened and the urchin hurried across to our table. "Word from fatso," said the lad. "'The birds have returned' – whatever that means."

"Capital!" said Holmes and, tipping the lad a further crown, we hurried from the café.

Never had my nerves been in such a state on approaching the familiar portals of 221B! My heart was pounding as we climbed the steps and Holmes rapped upon the door.

In due course Mrs Hudson answered the summons, and my heart leapt at the sight of her homely visage. She took in our disguise with evident distaste, until Holmes hurried forward, took her arm, and whispered, "Not a word, Mrs H! It is I, and my companion is Dr Watson."

She looked flummoxed. "But, but..." she wavered, gesturing at the stares. "Not twenty minutes ago, you..."

"All will be explained in due course," Holmes said. "Now, wait here until I give further word."

She nodded and backed against the wall. "Whatever you say, Mr Holmes."

I smiled at her as I passed, and followed Holmes up the staircase to our rooms.

He paused outside the living room door, and his long fingers wrapped themselves around the handle. With his right hand he drew the electrical gun, nodding at me to do the same.

With trembling fingers I pulled the weapon from my pocket and readied myself for action.

"After three," his whispered. "One... two... three. Now."

He opened the door and burst into the room.

A strange sight greeted us. I had expected the pair to leap into action, to counter our insurgence with an attack of their own – if not with weapons, then with main force. I had levelled my electrical gun in readiness, but lowered it as I beheld the scene before us.

The simulacrum of Sherlock Holmes sat bolt upright in his seat before the empty hearth, and across from him, in his own seat – for all the world like a matching book-end – sat the exact copy of myself. They did not move a muscle at our entry, did not so much as bat an eyelid.

Holmes approached his own simulacrum, weapon at the ready, and I stepped cautiously towards the second.

"In a state of quiescence," Holmes whispered. "Eerie, is it not?"

"Fair gives me the heebie-jeebies," I allowed.

"Well, it certainly makes our task all the easier," said he.

We should have known that it could not be the turkey shoot that Holmes had so optimistically forecast. No sooner than his words were out, and he was raising the gun towards the head of his own simulacrum, than the latter moved with lightning speed.

He leapt from the chair, dived at Holmes, and had his fingers about my friend's neck, in the process dashing the electrical gun from his grip.

At the same time, 'Watson' sprang into action. However, more through good fortune than intent, I backed off a yard, tripped up and in so doing accidentally fired off my weapon. With providence that to this day I find frightening to dwell upon – for what might our fates have been had my shot missed? – the electrical charge hit the advancing simulacrum squarely in the chest and sent it reeling backwards. It hit the wall and slid to the floor, quite dead.

Meanwhile, Holmes and his own mechanical copy were rolling around the floor, the simulacrum's grip upon my friend's throat tightening all the while, Holmes' face a shade of puce as the life was forced out of him. For one second, as he lay on his back, his bulging eyes found mine and implored me to do something.

I raised my gun, waited until the pair had completed another full roll, and in so doing bringing the simulacrum's back towards me, then fired. The mechanical man arched with a strangled cry, then spasmed and released its grip on my friend.

Holmes struggled coughing from under the dead weight and I, half delirious with relief, looked down upon the result of my handiwork.

"Sharp shooting, Watson. I owe you my life."

"Think nothing of it, Holmes. All in the line of duty, what?"

Holmes fell to examining the simulacra, declaring from time to time that he found the mechanical men fascinating.

"That's all very well, Holmes, but how the deuce are we going to go about getting rid of the pair."

Holmes looked up at me. "Get rid of them? Why, they will occupy my working hours for weeks, if not months. We will keep them in the storeroom, along with my stock of chemicals and other paraphernalia, and I will experiment upon them at my leisure. There is much to be learned, Watson, which will no doubt assist us in our fight against the Martian foe."

He stood, moved to the window and stared out. High above Regent's Park, dominating the sky-line, stood a Martian tripod – a symbol of all that was evil and malodorous about our overlords.

"We face a stern challenge in the years ahead, my friend. A terrible tide of evil has swept the shores of our world, an evil which knows no bounds and thinks itself unassailable – but, with courage, fortitude and ingenuity, I believe in time that we can overcome that tide, repel the invaders, and once again reclaim what is rightfully ours."

Coda

Later that afternoon, with the bodies of the simulacra safely stowed away and Mrs Hudson apprised of the situation and sworn to silence, we were taking a well-earned pot of tea when the telephone bell rang.

Holmes crossed the room and snatched up the receiver. "Yes?"

A tinny voice sounded, the words indistinct.

"That is correct," said Holmes, and then, "My word... Yes, yes, of course."

More words issued from the caller.

"We would be more than delighted. Yes, by all means. In thirty minutes, then." He replaced the receiver and stood a while in silent reflection.

"Who was that, Holmes?"

He turned and gave me a rare smile. "An agent of the rebel Martians," he said. "I was expecting a summons, of course, but not quite so soon. We have been called to the Lyons' tea-rooms, Piccadilly, at four o'clock."

At three-thirty we took an electrical cab to the heart of London; Holmes was uncommonly silent for the duration of the journey, no doubt contemplating the many trials and tribulations that awaited us. I, for my part, was equally sombre: we might have vanquished two defenceless simulacra in our rooms, but that was a small fight compared to that which lay ahead.

We alighted outside the tea-rooms, and before we crossed the pavement Holmes restrained me with a hand upon my arm. I looked up, at the louring cowl of the Martian tripod that defaced the Piccadilly sky-line – but it was not this that had caused my friend to pause.

He said, "What happened on Mars hit you hard, my friend."

I smiled bleakly. "Quite knocked the stuffing out of me, old man. I know we must fight on, and I will do, Holmes – as much in her memory as for ourselves, but it will be a melancholy..."

He stopped me. He was smiling. He said, "Don't be so downhearted, Watson. All is not as it appears."

"What?"

"Prepare yourself for a shock, or rather a surprise..."

"What the blazes do you mean, Holmes?"

"I mean," said he, "that it is not only the equatorial Martians who possess the means to manufacture the simulacra."

I blinked. "I don't quite follow..."

"The rebel Martians, our comrades in this battle, not only have the means to create simulacra, but have done so."

"Very well. That's good to know, but...?"

"Watson, you can be so slow at times!" Holmes laughed. "The rebels recruited humans to their cause. Not only that, but when an agent proved exceptional in the field, they created valuable simulacra so that these individuals might work as flight crew on the Martian ships to keep tabs on which humans were being lured to the Red Planet, while their originals remained to rouse the troops, as it were, on Earth."

"Good God, man!" I felt a little dizzy. His grip steadied me. "You mean to say...?"

He steered me across the pavement and into the tea-rooms. "That phone call was from her," he said – and he pointed across the room to where an uncommonly beautiful woman sat, recognisable to me despite her raven-haired disguise. "Miss Freya Hadfield-Bell," he went on, "the *original*."

In a daze, hardly able to believe my eyes, I crossed the room.

Hadfield-Bell rose, smiling at my speechlessness, and reached out to take my hand.

"Why..." I said, and, "Upon my word..." I gripped her hand and kissed her knuckles, tears springing to my eyes.

"I have heard reports of your bravery on Mars, Dr Watson, Mr Holmes," she said as we took our seats.

"Forgive me," I said. "This is something of a shock, a most wonderful shock, I might add. I thought you dead – indeed I saw you die with my own eyes!"

"My hapless simulacrum, Dr Watson," she murmured. "*I* live to fight another day, though from now on – given that our foe is aware of my direct involvement – with somewhat greater circumspection, and in disguise. And I am gratified that you two stalwarts will be joining me in the fight."

The thought of the battle ahead now swelled my heart, and it was all I could do to restrain myself from taking the woman in my arms.

"And now, my friends," she said, "I would like to hear, if you please, all about your – *our* – derring-do on Mars, sparing me no detail."

And so, beginning on the morning of our summons to investigate a spurious murder on Mars, I regaled Miss Hadfield-Bell with a full record of our many and various adventures on the Red Planet, which turbulent account I have now brought to a close.

About the Author

Eric Brown has won the British Science Fiction Award twice for his short stories, and his novel *Helix Wars* was shortlisted for the 2012 Philip K. Dick award. He has published sixty books, the latest of which include the crime novel *Murder Take Three*, the short story collection *Microcosms*, co-authored with Tony Ballantyne, and the novel *Binary System*. He has also written a dozen books for children and over a hundred and forty short stories. He writes a regular science fiction review column for the *Guardian* newspaper and lives in Cockburnspath, Scotland. His website can be found at:

www.ericbrown.co.uk

Also by Eric Brown

Strange Visitors

Eric Brown has been writing first rate science fiction for more than a quarter of a century, with over a hundred and twenty short stories, twenty-odd novels, several collections and no few novellas to his credit. *Strange Visitors* contains nine of those stories, none of them previously collected, plus a brand new piece written especially for this collection. Sit back, put your feet up, and immerse yourself in the rich worlds of Eric's imagination...

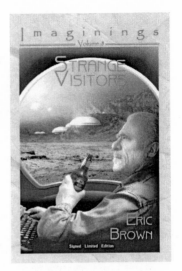

Starship Fall

David Conway leads an idyllic life on the colony world of Chalcedony, but all that changes when the mysterious holo star Carlotta Chakravorti-Luna enters his life and his alien friend Kee heads inland to take part in a potentially fatal Ashentay ritual. What follows is a convoluted and poignant tragedy which entangles Conway and his friends. In *Starship Fall*, Eric Brown has crafted a powerful, moving novella about friendship, love, and destiny.

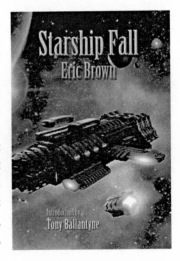

NewCon Press
Novellas

Set 1: *Cover art by Chris Moore*

1. The Iron Tactician – Alastair Reynolds
2. At the Speed of Light – Simon Morden
3. The Enclave – Anne Charnock
4. The Memoirist – Neil Williamson

All novellas are available separately in paperback edition and as a numbered limited edition hardback, signed by the author.

Each set of four novellas is also available as a limited edition lettered slipcase set, containing all four signed hardbacks with the combined artwork as a wrap-around.

Slipcase Set 1: [Sold Out]
Slipcase Set 2: [Sold Out]
Slipcase Set 3: £85.00   www.newconpress.co.uk

NEWCON PRESS

Publishing quality Science Fiction, Fantasy, Dark Fantasy and Horror for ten years and counting.

Winner of the 2010 'Best Publisher' Award from the European Science Fiction Society.

Anthologies, novels, short story collections, novellas, paperbacks, hardbacks, signed limited editions, e-books... Why not take a look at some of our other titles?

Featured authors include:
Neil Gaiman, Brian Aldiss, Kelley Armstrong, Peter F. Hamilton, Alastair Reynolds, Stephen Baxter, Christopher Priest, Tanith Lee, Joe Abercrombie, Dan Abnett, Nina Allan, Sarah Ash, Neal Asher, Tony Ballantyne, James Barclay, Chris Beckett, Lauren Beukes, Aliette de Bodard, Chaz Brenchley, Keith Brooke, Eric Brown, Pat Cadigan, Jay Caselberg, Ramsey Campbell, Simon Clark, Michael Cobley, Genevieve Cogman, Storm Constantine, Hal Duncan, Jaine Fenn, Paul di Filippo, Jonathan Green, Jon Courtenay Grimwood, Frances Hardinge, Gwyneth Jones, M. John Harrison, Amanda Hemingway, Paul Kane, Leigh Kennedy, Nancy Kress, Kim Lakin-Smith, David Langford, Alison Littlewood, Sarah Lotz, James Lovegrove, Una McCormack, Ian McDonald, Sophia McDougall, Gary McMahon, Ken MacLeod, Ian R MacLeod, Gail Z. Martin, Juliet E. McKenna, John Meaney, Simon Morden, Mark Morris, Anne Nicholls, Stan Nicholls, Marie O'regan, Philip Palmer, Stephen Palmer, Sarah Pinborough, Gareth L. Powell, Robert Reed, Rod Rees, Andy Remic, Mike Resnick, Mercurio D. Rivera, Adam Roberts, Justina Robson, Lynda E. Rucker, Stephanie Saulter, Gaie Sebold, Robert Shearman, Sarah Singleton, Martin Sketchley, Michael Marshall Smith, Kari Sperring, Brian Stapleford, Charles Stross, Tricia Sullivan, E.J. Swift, David Tallerman, Adrian Tchaikovsky, Steve Rasnic Tem, Lavie Tidhar, Lisa Tuttle, Simon Kurt Unsworth, Ian Watson, Freda Warrington, Liz Williams, Neil Williamson, and many more.

Join our mailing list to get advance notice of new titles and special offers:
www.newconpress.co.uk

IMMANION PRESS

Purveyors of Speculative Fiction

The Lightbearer by Alan Richardson

Michael Horsett parachutes into Occupied France before the D-Day Invasion. He is dropped in the wrong place, miles from the action, badly injured, and totally alone. He falls prey to two Thelemist women who have awaited the Hawk God's coming, attracts a group of First World War veterans who rally to what they imagine is his cause, is hunted by a troop of German Field Police who are desperate to find him, and has a climactic encounter with a mutilated priest who believes that Lucifer Incarnate has arrived...

The Lightbearer is a unique gnostic thriller, dealing with the themes of Light and Darkness, Good and Evil, Matter and Spirit.

"The Lightbearer is another shining example of Alan Richardson's talent as a story-teller. He uses his wide esoteric knowledge to produce a story that thrills, chills and startles the reader as it radiates pure magical energy. An unusual and gripping war story with more facets than a star sapphire." – Mélusine Draco, author of "Aubry's Dog" and "Black Horse, White Horse". ISBN: 978-1-907737-63-3 £11.99 $18.99

Dark in the Day, Ed. by Storm Constantine & Paul Houghton

Weirdness lurks beyond the margins of the mundane, emerging to dismantle our assumptions of reality. Dark in the Day is an anthology of weird fiction, penned by established writers and also those new to the genre – the latter being authors who are, or were, students of Creative Writing at Staffordshire University, where editor Storm Constantine occasionally delivers guest lectures. Her co-editor, Paul Houghton, is the senior lecturer in Creative Writing at the university.

Contributors include: Martina Bellovičová, J. E. Bryant, Glynis Charlton, Storm Constantine, Louise Coquio, Elizabeth Counihan, Krishan Coupland, Elizabeth Davidson, Siân Davies, Paul Finch, Rosie Garland, Rhys Hughes, Kerry Fender, Andrew Hook, Paul Houghton, Tanith Lee, Tim Pratt, Nicholas Royle, Michael Marshall Smith, Paula Wakefield, Ian Whates and Liz Williams.
ISBN: 978-1-907737-74-9 £11.99, $18.99

34 by Tanith Lee (writing as Esther Garber)

Tanith Lee 'co-wrote' *34* with Esther Garber – a fictional character (perhaps?). This is Esther's autobiography – but how much of it is true? Are her recollections of her unusual childhood in Egypt correct? And what of the mysterious 'gentleman', who Esther meets in France after having run away from home, who initiates her into forbidden pleasures of a Sapphic kind? Is she haunted or merely manipulated? Is she in love or simply obsessed? After one night of passion, Esther pursues her elusive tormentor into what seems to be a fairy-tale version of the French countryside, to journey's end and revelation, but also further mystery. Sensual, thought-provoking, and with an unreliable narrator, who twists and turns within her own tortured story, *34* demonstrates that haunting comes in many forms. As does desire. This new edition also includes the author's essay, on her work with Esther and Judas Garber: 'Meeting the Garbers'. ISBN: 978-1-907737-82-4 £10.99 $13.99

A Raven Bound with Lilies by Storm Constantine

Androgynous, and stronger in mind and body than humans, sometimes deadly, and often possessing unearthly beauty, the Wraeththu have captivated readers since Storm Constantine's first novel, *The Enchantments of Flesh and Spirit*, was published in 1988, regarded as ground-breaking in its treatment of gender and sexuality. This anthology of 15 tales collects all her published Wraeththu short stories into one volume, and also includes extra material, including the author's first explorations of the androgynous race. The tales range from the 'creation story' *Paragenesis*, through the bloody, brutal rise of the earliest tribes, and on into a future, where strange mutations are starting to emerge from hidden corners of the earth. With sumptuous illustrations by official Wraeththu artist Ruby, as well as pictures from Danielle Lainton and the author herself, *A Raven Bound with Lilies* is a must for any Wraeththu enthusiast, and is also a comprehensive introduction to the mythos for those who are new to it. ISBN: 978-1-907737-80-0 £11.99, $15.50

Immanion Press
http://www.immanion-press.com
info@immanion-press.com

CPSIA information can be obtained
at www.ICGtesting.com
Printed in the USA
FSOW01n0713050318
45318FS